The Women Who Got Away

JOHN UPDIKE

The Women Who Got Away

GREAT LOVES

PENGUIN BOOKS

Published by the Penguin Group
Penguin Books Ltd, 80 Strand, London WC2R 0RL, England
Penguin Group (USA) Inc., 375 Hudson Street, New York, New York 10014, USA
Penguin Group (Canada), 90 Eglinton Avenue East, Suite 700, Toronto, Ontario, Canada M4P 2Y3
(a division of Pearson Penguin Canada Inc.)
Penguin Ireland, 25 St Stephen's Green, Dublin 2, Ireland
(a division of Penguin Books Ltd)
Penguin Group (Australia), 250 Camberwell Road, Camberwell, Victoria 3124, Australia
(a division of Pearson Australia Group Pty Ltd)
Penguin Books India Pvt Ltd, 11 Community Centre, Panchsheel Park, New Delhi – 110 017, India
Penguin Group (NZ), 67 Apollo Drive, Rosedale, North Shore 0632, New Zealand
(a division of Pearson New Zealand Ltd)
Penguin Books (South Africa) (Pty) Ltd, 24 Sturdee Avenue,
Rosebank, Johannesburg 2196, South Africa

Penguin Books Ltd, Registered Offices: 80 Strand, London WC2R 0RL, England

www.penguin.com

'Transaction' first published in *Oui* and in *The Early Stories 1953–1975*, published in the
United States of America by Alfred A. Knopf, Inc. 2003
The Early Stories 1953–1975 first published in Great Britain by Hamish Hamilton 2004
'Natural Color', 'New York Girl' and 'The Women Who Got Away' first published in *Licks of
Love*, published in the United States of America by Alfred A. Knopf, Inc. 2000
'Licks of Love in the Heart of the Cold War' first appeared in *The Atlantic Monthly* and
Licks of Love, published in the United States of America by Alfred A. Knopf, Inc. 2000
Licks of Love first published in Great Britain by Hamilton Hamilton 2000
This selection published in Penguin Books 2007

1

Typeset by Rowland Phototypesetting Ltd, Bury St Edmunds, Suffolk
Printed in England by Clays Ltd, St Ives plc

978-0-141-03293-1

Contents

John Updike was born in 1932 in Shillington, Pennsylvania. He graduated from Harvard College in 1954, and spent a year in Oxford, England, at the Ruskin School of Drawing and Fine Art. From 1955 to 1957 he was a member of staff of *The New Yorker*; since 1957 he has lived in Massachusetts as a freelance writer. He is the author of more than twenty novels as well as numerous collections of short stories, poems and criticism. His novels have won the Pulitzer Prize (twice), the National Book Award, the National Book Critics Circle Award, the Rosenthal Award and the Howells Medal.

Natural Color

Frank saw her more than a block away, in the town where he had come to live, where Maggie had no business to be, and he no expectation of seeing her. Something about the way she held her head, as if she were marvelling at the icicled eaves of the downtown shops, sparked recognition. Or perhaps it was the way the low winter sun caught the red of her hair, so it glinted like a signal. His wife used to doubt aloud that the color was natural, and he had had to repress the argument that if Maggie dyed it she dyed her pubic hair to match. It was true, Maggie considered her hair a glory. When she let it down, the sheaves of it became an enveloping, entangling third presence in the bed, and when it was pinned up, as it was today, her head looked large and her neck poignantly thin, at its cocky tilt.

She was with a man – a man taller than she, though she was herself tall. He moved beside her with a bear-like protective shuffle, half sideways, so as not to miss a word she was tossing out, her naked hands gesturing in the February sun. Frank remembered her face whitened by shock and wet with tears. Each word he reluctantly pulled from himself had been a blow deepening her pallor, driving her deeper into defeat.

'I can't swing it,' he had said, with both their households in turmoil and the town around them scandalized.

'You mean,' she said, her face furrowed, her upper lip tense in her effort to have utter clarity at this moment, 'you want to go back?'

'I don't want to, exactly, but I think I should.'

'Then go, Frank. Go, darling. It makes it simpler for me, in a way.'

He had thought that a lovely, pathetic bit of female bravado, an attempt to match rejection with rejection, but in fact she had carried through with her divorce, whereas he had kept his family intact and had moved to another town. That had been over twenty years ago. The children he had decided not to leave had eventually grown up and left home. The wife he had clung to had maintained a self-preserving detachment, which as they together advanced into middle age became a decided distance, maintained with dry humor and an impervious dignity. He had opted for a wife, and a wife she was, no less or more.

As for Maggie, she had recovered; she had a companion, and at a distance looked smart, in a puffy pea-green parka and black pants that made her legs appear theatrically long. Shocked by the spark glinting from her hair, Frank ducked into the nearest door, that of the drugstore, to spare himself the impact of a confrontation, of introductions and chatter. It was somehow an attack on him, to have her striding about so boldly in his town.

While he roamed the drugstore aisles as if looking for a magic medication or a perfect birthday card, he slowly filled with fury at her, for going beyond him and making a life. Sexual jealousy of a wholly unreasonable sort raged in him as he blindly stalked between the cold tablets and the skin lotions, the sleeping pills and stomach-acid neutralizers. He skimmed the array of condoms, displayed, in this progressive, AIDS-wary age, like a rack of many-colored candies, each showing on the box a shadowy man and woman bending their heads conspiratorially close. It occurred to him, as his blood pounded, that sex has very little to do with kindness. He had been rough with Maggie, cruel, in the heat of their affair. It had been his first, but not hers. She had told him in the front seat of his car, with that serious, concentrating stare of hers, 'That time when Sam and I were separated, I was an absolute whore. I'd sleep with *any*body.'

The sweeping solemnity of the confession would have made him smile, had he not been awed by the grandeur of her promiscuity as he tried to imagine it. She seemed to swell in size, there beside him in the front seat of his Ford station wagon, parked on a dead-end lane between towns. That early-spring meeting, hurriedly arranged by phone, was like an interview, she in winter tweeds from shopping in Boston, he in his business suit. He didn't ask for details. She volunteered a ski instructor in Vermont, a scuba instructor in the Caribbean – handsome, carefree young fishers of women. She didn't say if she had slept with any of their neighbors, but he imagined some, and thus his heart was hardened before their own affair had begun. He was obliged to sleep with her now. It was a kind of race, in which he had fallen dangerously behind. The men she had slept with were each still in her, a kind of investment, generating interest while he had been chastely admiring her from afar. Part of Frank's gift to her was the heightened value that his innocence had assigned her. Because she was so experienced, they were never quite equal. She ran risks, coming to him, the same risks he did, of discovery and a disrupted family, but he considered her marriage too damaged already to grieve for, whereas his own was enhanced by his betrayal, his wife and children rendered precious in their vulnerability. Returning to them, damp and panting from his sins, he nearly wept at their sweet ignorance. Yet he couldn't stop. He led Maggie on, addicted to her and careless of their fate, until the time came to disentangle his fate from hers. She herself had said it: 'You're *hard* on me, Frank.'

He thought she might mean just the vigor of his love-making. They were both in a sweat, in her sunny bed with its view of a horse-farm riding ring, and she, underneath him, was doubly drenched. They had begun seeing each other in April; they were discovered and cut off before autumnal weather arrived. He re-membered her in bright cotton frocks, animated at parties afloat in summer lightness, all her animation secretly directed at him. She was warm with Ann, his wife, and he was hearty with Sam, her husband, though even here there was inequality. She seemed genuinely to like Ann and, when with Frank, would wonder aloud how he could ever think of leaving his lovely wife. Each tryst, on the other hand, strengthened his impression that Sam – big, red-faced, his heavy head lowered with clumsy, shortsighted menace – was unworthy of her, and her remaining in her marriage was a sign of weakness, a meek acceptance of daily pollution.

'You have anything better to offer?' Maggie had once challenged him, having pinched her lips together and decided to take the leap. Her eyes in this moment of daring had been round, like a child's.

He felt attenuated, strained, answering weakly, 'You know I'd love to be your husband. If I weren't already somebody else's.'

'The beautiful prisoner,' she said, gazing off as if suddenly bored. 'I do think we should stop seeing each other.'

'Oh my God, no. I'll die.'

'Well, it's killing me. You're not being mature. When a gentleman has had his fun with a lady, he takes his leave.'

He hated it when she pulled sexual rank on him. He wanted to learn but not to be instructed. 'Is that how Sam would act?'

'Sam's not so bad as you think,' she said, brushing away, with a sudden awkward hiding motion, tears that had started to her eyes, sprung by some image touched within the tense works of this suspended situation.

'Good in bed,' Frank suggested, hating the two of them. In bed: this very bed, with its view of trim stables and fenced pastures.

She ignored the jealous probe. She said, reflecting, 'He has a sense of me that's not entirely off. In his coarse way, he has manners.'

'And I don't?'

'Frank,' she exclaimed in an exasperation that still let the tears stand in her eyes. 'Why does everything always have to come back to you?'

'Because,' he could have answered, 'you have made me love myself.' But there were many things he could have said to Maggie, before communications between them suddenly ceased, Sam blundering in with bullish fury and lawyerly threats, Ann receding with a beautiful wounded pride. Frank found himself Maggie's enemy, having failed to become her husband.

In the freezing winter and raw spring before he and his family had moved from that town to this one, six miles distant, there was a long social season in which they all continued to rotate in each other's vicinity. Sam moved to a bachelor rental in a neighboring town three miles away, not so far as to be out of reach of sympathetic gestures from their large communal acquaintance. Frank and Ann hunkered down in embattled, recriminatory renewal of their vows, mixed with spells of humorous weariness. And Maggie found herself marooned in her big house with the two children, an eight-year-old girl and a six-year-old boy. Their formerly shared friends, forced to choose among these explosive elements, opted for the intact couple over the separated one. Sam, though his face seemed redder than ever and his eyes were narrowed as if his face had been pummelled, established himself as willing to co-exist in the same room with Frank, and even to exchange a few forced courtesies. But Ann fled the one occasion, the annual Christmas-carol sing in the historical-society mansion, where Maggie had dared appear. Maggie showed up late, in a dazzling sequined long-sleeved green top and a scarlet velvet skirt. Frank smiled at the audacity of the outfit; Ann gave a whimper and whirled from the room, straight down the hallway, hung with old daguerreotypes, toward the front door, prized for its exemplary Federalist moldings and fine leaded fanlight. Chasing her out with their coats into the cold, Frank said, 'That was a cruel thing to do.'

'Not as cruel as trying to steal my husband.'

'That isn't what she tried.'

'Well, what did she try? Fucking as a spiritual exercise?'

'Please, Ann. People are looking out of the windows.' Though in fact the choruses of 'Good King Wenceslas' rolled obliviously out the tall windows onto the snowy sidewalk. The town had seen worse spats than theirs, including a Unitarian-Congregationalist church schism in the 1820s. 'Put on your coat,' he said stiffly, and led her by the arm to where their car was parked, the station wagon in which Maggie had solemnly told him she had been an absolute whore, but whose interior now was awash in the childish odor of candy-bar crumbs and spilled milkshakes. In truth, the marriage had in the short run fattened on the affair: Ann was impressed that he had made a conquest of the spectacular Maggie, and Frank was moved by his cool wife's flare of jealous passion. It was as if Maggie, in her bereft, ostracized state, were a prize they had jointly dragged home. 'If you can't hold it together in public,' he told her, 'it means she can't go anywhere where you're apt to be.'

'We're *try*ing to get out of town, we've got realtors coming out of our *ears*,' Ann said with comical vehemence. 'I'm *damned* if I'm going to take the children out of school before it ends in May. They're heart-broken we're moving in any case.' As the car heater warmed, drowning in its gases the sour-milkshake scent, and the rumpled blocks of the old town rolled by, she conceded, 'I'm sorry. That was not a good-sport thing to do. But just seeing her physically, after talking about her for weeks and weeks, it came over me how you'd seen her . . . how you knew every . . . and she looked so great, actually, in that grotesque outfit.' Ann went on, 'Pale and tense, but it's taken a few pounds off her. Wish I could say the same.'

He reached over and squeezed her plump thigh through the thickness of her winter coat. 'Different styles,' he said, obliquely bragging. They were united, it seemed to him, in admiration of Maggie – two suppliants bowed beneath a natural force. Though rapprochement on such a basis was bound to decay, for a time it made for a conspiratorial closeness.

In the meantime, Maggie was crossed off party lists. She pursued her daily duties in majestic isolation, visited by only a few gossip-hungry women and oddball men sensing an opportunity. Frank was divided between acquiescence in her exclusion – her power over him, the grandeur she had for him, left no room for pity – and an impossible wish to reunite, to say the words to her that would lift them above it all and put them back in bed together. More experienced than he, she knew there were no such words. A few months after the Christmas-carol sing, the town fathers sponsored an Easter-egg hunt on the sloping common, this side of the cemetery. In the milling about, while parents chased after frantic, scooting children on the muddy brown grass, he managed to sidle up to Maggie, in her friendly spring tweeds. She gave him an unamused stare and said to him, as if the words had been stored up, 'Your wife has ruined my social life. And my children's. Sam is furious.'

Such a petty, specific grievance seemed astonishingly unworthy of them and their love. Startled, Frank said, 'Ann doesn't scheme. She just lets things happen.' As if, after all this silence between them, they had met to debate his wife's character. Maggie turned away. Sick with the rejection, he admired the breadth of her shoulders and the wealth of her hair, done up in a burnished, glistening French twist.

To a tourist travelling through, one New England town looks much like another – white spire, green common, struggling little downtown – but they have considerable economic and spiritual differences, and their citizens know what they are. Frank and Ann had, after a six-month struggle with real-estate agents, moved to a town where the property lines were marked by walls and hedges and No Trespassing signs. The friends they slowly made were generally older than they, a number of them widowed or retired. The lives, the winterized

summer houses, the grounds maintained by lawn ser-
vices were all in a state of finish. The town they had
moved from had been a work in progress, with crooked
streets laid out by Puritan footsteps and boundary lines
marked by lost boulders and legendary trees whose
stumps had rotted to nothing. The young householders
had tried to do their own maintenance, leaving ladders
leaning against porch roofs and two sides of a house
unpainted until next summer. The yards were hard-
used by packs of children; there was a constant coming
and going of Saturday-afternoon tennis or touch foot-
ball turning into drinks before everyone rushed home
to shower and shave for that night's dinner party. You
lived in other people's houses as much as you could;
there was an ache to being in your own, a nagging
unsuppressible suspicion that happiness was elsewhere.
Driving back from taking the babysitter home, Frank
would pass darkened houses where husbands he knew
were lying in bed, head to murmuring head, with wives
he coveted.

Out of this weave of promiscuous friendship, this
confusedly domestic scrimmage, Maggie had emerged,
touching his hip with hers as they stood side by side at
a lawn party's busy, linen-clad bar, or exclaiming, in an
involuntary, almost fainting little-girl voice, 'Oh, don't
go!' when he and Ann stood up at last to leave a dinner
party that she and Sam had given. And when, at one
of the suburban balls with which the needs of charity
dotted the calendar, his turn came to dance with
Maggie, they nestled as close as the sanction of alcohol
allowed, and at the end she gave his hand a sharp,

stern, quite sober squeeze. It took very clear signals to burn through his fog of shyness and connubial inertia, but she had enough expertise to know that, once ignited, he would blaze.

How gentle and patient, in retrospect, her initiation of him had been. Their meetings took place mostly in her house, because Sam worked in Boston and Ann didn't. Frank remembered, rounding the rack of condoms into a realm of packaged antihistamine capsules, how the driveway of her house, which sat on the edge of town, next to a horse farm and riding stable, was hidden behind a tilting tall stockade-style fence and a mass of overgrown lilacs. Sam would talk of replacing the fence and pruning the lilacs but didn't do it that summer. Approaching, Frank needed to slow for the hairpin turn into the driveway; it was a dangerous moment when his car might have been recognized on the road – several of their friends' children took riding lessons – and he would hold his breath as, half hidden behind the great straggly lilacs, he would glide across the crackling gravel and into the garage. Maggie would have swung up the garage door for him, which took some strength in this era before electronic controls. She would be waiting for him behind the connecting door into the kitchen, in a bathing suit or less. His eyes would still be adjusting from sunlight. She would bound into his arms like a long, smooth, shivering puppy. He stared at the Sudafed and Contac, his whole body swollen by a stupid indignation at having lost all that.

*

At last, making a few distracted purchases by way of paying for the shelter, he dared leave the drugstore. He looked down the street and saw with relief that the vista of icicled shops held no red glint. Heart pounding, as if he were being pursued by an enemy, he made his way to his car and returned to his house. It was a weather-tight box, a well-built tract house on a two-acre square of land. The foundation-masking shrubs newly planted when they moved in now looked over-grown, crowding the brick steps and front windows. In the kitchen, Ann, in her old loden coat, was un-packing bags of groceries into the refrigerator; her face as she turned to him wore a slant expression, brimming with wary mischief. 'I saw an old friend of yours in the Stop & Shop.' The giant bright super-market was part of a mall that had arisen in the farm country, slowly going under to development, between the town they had left and the town where they lived.

'Who?' he asked, though from the peculiar liveliness of her expression he had already guessed.

'Maggie Linsford. Or whatever her name is now.' Maggie had taken back her maiden name after her divorce from Sam, and Ann could never be bothered to remember it.

'Chase,' Frank said. 'Unless she's remarried.'

'She wouldn't do that to you. What's in that bag in your hand?'

'Razor blades. Sudafed. And I got you some of that perfumed French bath gel you like. "*Dorlotez-vous*," the label says.'

'How sweet and silly of you. I have scads of it. Don't you want to hear about Maggie?'

'Sure.'

'She was with this man, she introduced him, in that rather grand way she has, as "my friend." He reminded me of Sam – big and red-faced and take-charge.'

'Good.'

'Frank, don't look so sick. You're thinking back twenty-five years.'

'No, I was thinking about "take-charge." I guess he was. Did she seem pleasant?'

'Oh, effusive. I always liked her, until you came between us. And she me, no?'

He wondered. At the height of their affair their spouses had seemed small and pathetic beneath them, like field mice under a hawk, virtually too small to discuss. 'Sure,' he said. 'She admired you very much. She couldn't understand what I saw in her.'

'Don't be sarcastic. You're no fun, Frank. I bring you this goodie, and you look constipated.'

'What did the two of you discuss, effusively?'

'Oh, winter. Food. The appallingness of malls. Apparently a new one is going in on the land of the old riding stable next to that place she had with Sam. She complained there wasn't any gluten-free flour or low-fat cookies in the whole supermarket – maybe she's trying to slim down her beefy friend – and I told her we had a new health-food store just open up here, a charming idealistic girl we were all trying to give business to. She said she'd drive right over. If you were hanging out in the drugstore, I'm surprised you didn't see her.'

He saw he must confess; there was no evading feminine intuition. 'I did. I saw this flash of red hair down below the post office, and ducked into the drugstore rather than talk to her.'

'Frank dear, how silly again. She would have been nothing but pleasant, I'm sure.'

'I didn't like the look of the thug she was with.'

'If she had been alone, would you have gone up to her?'

'I doubt it.'

Ann put the last package into the refrigerator and closed the door, hard enough so that a magnet in the shape of a pineapple fell to the floor. She didn't pick it up. 'Your reacting so skittishly doesn't speak very well for *us*.'

Infidelity, he reflected, widens a couple's erotic field at first, but leaves it weaker and frazzled in the end. Like a mind-expanding drug, it destroys cells. He told Ann, 'I felt nothing. I felt repelled.'

'A "flash of red hair" – I'll say. She's dyeing it an impossible color these days.'

'You always said she dyed it.'

'And she always did. Certainly now.'

'I don't think so. Not Maggie.'

'Oh, you poor thing, her hair would be as gray as yours and mine if she didn't dye it. She looked cheap, cheap and whorish, which is something I couldn't have honestly said before. You were smart not to allow yourself a look up close.'

'You bitch, I know Maggie's hair better than you do.' Ann froze, not certain from his expression whether or not he would come forward and strike her; but she was safe, he was not even seeing her. The woman he did see, stepping naked toward him across a sun-striped carpet, was the one who, as long as he loved her, he must hate.

New York Girl

In those days New York seemed as far from Buffalo as Singapore does now. I used to take the train, all eight stultifying hours of it, or drive, on Route 17, stopping off in Corning and Binghamton, where we had clients, and then coming down through the Catskills into Westchester County. I used to stay at the Roosevelt or the Biltmore, easy walks with a suitcase from Grand Central Station. Once you were in New York, you were on another planet, a far shore; it cried out for you to establish another life. Time, at home so filled with the needs of the house and of the children and of the wife – Carole kept counting her gray hairs, and childbearing had given her varicose veins – time was here your own, hours of it, and no one told you how to fill it, once the day's appointments had been kept. Extruded nonferrous metal, mainly aluminum alloy, was our product. Combination storm-window manufacturers were our big customers, but in the Sixties a sideline had developed in metal picture frames, and this brought me into contact with the lower echelons of the art world. I visited galleries to see what they needed, and in one of them, on an upper floor on West Fifty-seventh Street, I met Jane.

She wasn't plain, but she wasn't a conventional beauty either. There was something asymmetrical about her; not just her smile but her whole bony face, with its high cheekbones and powdered-over freckles, seemed a little tugged to one side. When she gestured, her arms and hands appeared too long, with an extra hinge to them somewhere. Her gestures involved a lot of sudden retraction and self-stroking, as if she were checking herself for loose parts. She kept flipping back her long ironed hair, a dull reddish color that reminded me of pencil shavings and the cedary fragrance that arises when you empty the sharpener. She wore a beige knit minidress and black pantyhose; her hips were wider and her thighs fuller than one would have expected from the bony top half of her body, and this added to her touching aura of being out of kilter, there in the merciless brightness of the display space. The white walls held hasty abstractions, blue pigments smeared upon white-primed canvas, all the same size and framed in thin cold-rolled steel, like a row of bathroom mirrors.

'I'm not here to look at the paintings,' I apologized. 'Just the frames. To get an idea of what you need.'

'I guess inconspicuous is what we need,' she said, fluttering one long hand at the cruel wall and then quickly resting the same hand on the ball of her shoulder and giving it a squeeze. 'A lot of the artists can't stand any frames, they say it creates a mind-set, they want it to look *rough*, and are fighting the rectangle in any case. But we find,' she said, relenting with a heart-catching crooked smile, 'the customers are reassured if there's a frame. It shows it's *finished*; the artist *means* it.'

'I'm interested more in the flanges,' I said, but she knew already that I was interested in her. I had gone stupid; a mist of a kind had arisen between us. In those benighted days such an interest was considered not an affront but a datum, to be factored into whatever one's life equation was at the time. Jane and I were both in our early thirties, a time for fresh calculations. Back in Buffalo I had survived, with my family, a tumultuous infatuation and explosive dénouement; in the aftermath I had adjusted downward my estimate of how much happiness I could extract from the world, and of how much I could offer any woman not my wife. I was wised-up and shy. But, then, New York was another world – an infinity of restaurants and apartments and elevator shafts and human appetites. I wasn't due home until late tomorrow night.

'For the flanges,' Jane said, after a gawky hesitation and an alarmed stare that for a second burned through the mist, 'you maybe need to come into the storage room.' There, in a crammed but not totally disorderly clutter of unframed art and unassembled frames, of T-squares and knives and a scarred worktable, we sat on tippy tall stools and each smoked a cigarette.

'What do *you* do, Stan?'

I described my job, as a would-be engineer turned salesman of alloy extrusions. I described my eight-room house, my three-child family, my two-car garage in Eggertsville, and the new red Toro snow-blower with which I tried to keep a path open through the fabled snows off Lake Erie. 'Now tell me about you.'

She smoked like someone who had never smoked

before, bringing the cigarette to her lips with a flattened hand, the fingers tensely curved backward. She stabbed out the butt in a clunky green ashtray as if she were crushing a stubbornly vital insect. 'No time for that, sweetie,' she said, dismounting from the stool with an awkward hop. Her shoes at the end of her long full-thighed legs were a startling shiny scarlet, like red nails on black fingers. 'I hear people out front. Maybe they're stealing the art. I ought to go encourage them.' She added, 'I have a child, too. A nine-year-old boy. No husband, no car, no snow-blower, but a dear hope-ful child.'

This time her hesitation and her stare had a clear import: it was my turn to make a move, and quickly. It was my turn to be awkward. 'Would you, would you like to have dinner tonight? Or do you have better things to do? I bet you do.'

Somewhat to my disappointment – I foresaw com-plications – she was not busy. 'Sounds good to me,' she said, brushing her hair back from one ear in a thought-ful way. 'How about to you? You don't sound too sure.'

'What about the boy?'

'I'll get a sitter.'

'Really? On such short notice?' In Buffalo, sitters were sullen pubescent girls, off in a fourteen-year-old's dream world, or else grandmotherly women, widows and spinsters, who were highly valued and had to be signed up weeks in advance. I did feel dubious, but the haze between us had thickened.

'Really,' she insisted. 'Eight o'clock too late for you?

I'll feed him and tuck him in. Here's the address – it's a walk from here. Don't be shy, Stan. It'll be fun.'

Jane lived on the West Side, twenty blocks north of where she worked. That night, or one not long there-after, I was amazed to discover that a number of cabs were cruising those streets at three in the morning. Stepping out onto Columbus Avenue, I had been fear-ful, just drowsily emerged from the warmth of her bed. Our whispers of farewell still hissed in my ears; her last kiss was evaporating under my nose. My whole body felt as defenseless as a slug's. I had left because of the boy, so he wouldn't find me there when he awoke, and because of my wife, who might have been telephoning the hotel, frantic with some domestic emergency. Carole had a nervous, clinging streak beneath her practical-minded aplomb. I had led her into multiple motherhood and then kept hitting the road.

Now I had my own emergency: the empty straight streets stretched to vanishing points all around me; a mugger – did we call them muggers then? – could have been waiting, switchblade ready, in any of the upright dark doorways, behind any of the brownstone stairs. But an all-night drug-store gleamed two blocks away, and fits of traffic animated the avenue. Within a minute or two, a taxi materialized with its roof light signalling rescue. The driver and I were usually chatty on these returns to my hotel; he was pleased to have a fare and my tongue was oiled by sexual triumph and a sense of escape. Those rides through the almost deserted city had a clean, clicking feeling: I was back on track.

Pulling up at the hotel, paying the cabdriver, walking in my warm dishevelment past the noncommittal desk clerk, into the elevator, down the windowless corridor, into the still, expectant room, I rejoined a self who had been here all along. The bed was cool and tightly made, with a mint on the pillow.

Sometimes Jane came to my hotel. Once, when I had left the room dark in anticipation of her arrival, she asked as I let her in, 'Is this where the orgy is?' Another time – the same time? how many times were there? – we couldn't open the door when it was time for her to leave. It was absurd and frightening; an invisible enforcer had trapped me with the living evidence of my crime. This was after 2:00 a.m., long past time for Jane to leave the orgy and to send the baby-sitter home. A woman in the apartment below would sit for her at short notice. A sisterhood of single New York women existed, egging each other on in the long-odds mating game. Men – useful, unattached, hetero-sexual men – were scarce, scarcer here than in the hinterlands; Jane taught me this to her disadvantage, for I rarely worried, in the months between my trips to the city, that she would not be there for me, as glamorous and game as ever.

The mystery of the locked room was never com-pletely solved. The moral standards of hotel manage-ment in those years of imminent sexual revolution were obscure to me; I stammered guiltily, calling the main desk. For what seemed many minutes of waiting, Jane and I were prisoners together, fully dressed and physi-cally weary. Finally, a black maintenance man turned the latch from the outside with a master key. He fiddled bemusedly with the obdurate inner knob and chatted with us as if we were the most ordinary, consecrated daylight couple who had ever required his expertise. We made a small society, at that odd hour; he and Jane hit it off, especially, vying in theories on the mechanical puzzle. She said, 'I thought it might be like a subway turnstile – you needed a token.' It was a revelation to me, this wee-hour camaraderie of New Yorkers, and the city's genial way of folding my adultery into its round-the-clock hustle.

Carole and I had met in college – the University of Buffalo, before its SUNY connection. A math major, she was bright, methodical, compact, and rounded. She had thick glasses and thin, serious lips. I saw at a glance that she would be a trustworthy partner and mother to my children. My estimate was sound; she was all I could reasonably ask for in a helpmeet. We both studied too hard for much of a formal courtship; we just palled around for two years and in senior year agreed to get married. So to stop at one of Manhattan's corner flower shops and buy an armful of red roses or lavender gladioli was to play a rôle, that of a swain, for the first time. I played opposite the veteran Italian actress behind the counter, with her faint mustache and frayed sweater and tightly wound iron-gray bun into which a yellow pencil had been thrust at a dramatic angle. In the burning limelight, all my senses were heightened a notch: I registered with a feverish keenness the petalled colors massed with their reflections in the black display

22

window, and the chill that wafted out of the glass-
doored refrigerator where the cut flowers were stored,
and the angry deft gesture with which my co-star
plucked the pencil from the back of her head and
scribbled the receipt before sending me out into the
street with my green-paper cone of blooms. Bearing
flowers enrolled me in the city's anonymous army of
lovers. A few bright doorways up Columbus Avenue,
I would stop at the liquor store for a quart of Wild
Turkey – the most expensive brand of bourbon within
my sense of possibilities. At home Carole and I drank
Jim Beam, and not much of it. But I was somebody
else here, a sugar daddy from Singapore. Flowers and
liquor – what else could I take Jane to clothe my
gratitude? Sex paid for, however inadequately, was
better – clearer, more naked, more of a rush – than
married sex that we expect to sneak up on us for free.
I did not drop in at the liquor store often enough –
four or five times a year – to warrant a greeting from
the dour brothers who owned it, but after a year I
could see something flicker across their wary faces,
a suspicion that they should know me, that I was
familiar. My courtship glow made me stand out, perhaps. I might have been a young husband, new to
the neighborhood and still dazzled by the delights of
cohabitation.

A surely imaginary happiness bathes my memories.
Once, in January, I stood at Jane's front windows
looking down at the tops of a row of buttonwoods as
a slanting wet snow laid crescents of white on each
little round pod, while the apartment at my back

overflowed with the plangent human pealing of the
Swingle Singers performing Bach fugues – a record
Jane had received at Christmas, I didn't ask from whom
– and I felt joy to the point of tears. My body, wrapped
in a loose wool bathrobe of hers, felt stuffed with the
spiritual woolliness of contentment. At my back, just
off the kitchen, she was setting up our breakfast. Para-
boloids of orange juice and a cylinder of marmalade
glowed with inner light. The scent of toasting English
muffins intersected the sight of the diagonal snow
adhering to the buttonwood pods. The morning
moment kept overflowing, on and on, Bach going at it
again and again, never getting enough. Jeffrey, Jane's
son, was with a friend or his father so that, this once,
we had the apartment to ourselves. I had spent the
night, daring the phone back at the hotel not to ring.
Jane was close enough to my size so that I could wear
her blue robe. I could never have gotten into a robe of
Carole's; she was petite and neat. What I loved in Jane
was her excess, her muchness – the hips so wide she
walked with a seesawing lurch, the cedary hair that was
always falling into my face, the angular downy arms,
the legs that stretched to the corners of the bed. It was
a single bed; we had slept badly, snoring in each other's
faces, dodging elbows.

Her ex-husband was an artist, not successful enough
to supply child support or for me to have heard of him
but not so unsuccessful that he had to abandon an
artistic image of himself. I hated and envied her world
of artists – their lofts and debauches, their self-
exemption from the ruck of ordinary labor, their other-

worldly charm. Jeffrey, nine and then ten, was doe-eyed and gravely polite, perhaps because I usually saw him when he was being put to bed, at the moment of my departure with his mother. His tiny room's one tall window looked south, upon the lights of midtown mounting in rectangular masses higher and higher – an Arabian Nights view that made me grateful almost to tears to have been granted a small illicit purchase upon such display, such splendor.

Jeffrey was precocious at school, and Jane was proud of that. Occasionally he and I talked; my impression was of a sly docility toward me, a guarded hope. His mother's loneliness was the air he breathed, and I gave him a brief change of air. He was blonder than she, English-looking, with a pointed chin and pale skin and rosy cheeks; only his owlish brown eyes and black eyebrows gave evidence of a darker strain, his father's. He had read lots of Tolkien and C. S. Lewis; at school he was having a little trouble with how to add unlike fractions. Of the men in the margin of his life I must have been the only one with a degree in engineering.

'You make the numbers so nicely!' he exclaimed, when I began to instruct him in common denominators.

'You've got to. If they're not clear they're worse than useless. That kind of "4" you make, with the closed top, looks too much like a "9."'

'But, Stan, the "4"s in books all are closed like that.'

'Books get away with a lot we can't get away with in real life,' I told him, paternally. It was enchanting, somehow, to be called 'Stan' by a child the age of my own children. I was momentarily a member of this family, but the membership was woven of angel hair, insubstantial, with none of the weight of real family ties. I was temporarily magical, to go with their magic, so precariously poised in mid-air here, between the tops of the buttonwood trees and the ranks of burning skyscraper lights.

Jane's apartment was furnished cheaply; unframed out-of-series prints were tacked to the walls, and instead of end tables she simply used stacks of art books and catalogues. I felt unprecedentedly nimble in this apartment, light-footed, stealthy, stealing happiness from these rooms and then gliding out the door, into the elevator (how loud its doors and gears seemed, in that solidly sleeping building!), and on to the barren streets that with mysterious quickness yielded a roaming cab, its third eye blazing.

Adventures! Adventures with Jane. We had to eat. After the maintenance man finally let us out of my hotel room, we were both famished and found an all-night Automat on East Forty-second Street. It was like entering a Hopper with a Petty girl on my arm. Escorting Jane into any restaurant felt luxurious. We never phoned ahead – I didn't like jostling with the fruity, accented voices at the name places, La Côte Basque and so on – but New York abounded with half-empty no-name restaurants where they were happy to see you; the maître d' beamed at the sight of Jane, in her miniskirt and falling cedar-red hair. I remember a pricy Swedish smorgasbord in the East

Fifties, and a steak place with Texas decor and big windows overlooking Third Avenue, and a fish place with wooden tables somewhere south of Washington Square. Broadway plays took too long to waste our precious time together on, but she did lead me to an 'underground' movie somewhere in the dreary Thirties, and to a play in the Village about a group of dope addicts sitting around waiting for their 'connection' to show up. I kept hugging her during the play; its message of hopelessness, of addiction, seemed to be directed at us, and to enlist us in the scattered troops of rebellion in those pre-Vietnam years. But she pointedly did not respond, as if asserting, while her straying hair tingled against my cheek, that my romantic sense of it all let me off too easily.

The art movie had no plot that I can remember; there was a lot of grainy slow panning and some jumpy surrealistic collage, including a quick, repeated act of fellatio that caused Jane to exclaim softly at my side, 'Uh-oh.' The act was faked with photographs of a dildo and a young woman's face, not matter-of-factly enacted for the camera as it would have been a few years later. For the time, it was daring, as was Jane when, in bed, not without awkwardness, she startled me by suddenly dipping her head to touch her lips to the tip of my erection, like a small girl yielding to the impulse to bestow a kiss on the bald head of a favorite doll. The kiss was quick and light and seemed to startle her as much as it did me; it remains in my mind an isolated moment, lit by a flower-shop glow – the moist sheltered intimacy, the expectant soft petals. I didn't press her to repeat the gesture; it had derived from an overflow of feeling I was in no position to force. I could take, but I couldn't demand.

What did she get from me? A lesson in chopsticks. We had wandered into a rather overdecorated, underlit Chinese restaurant on Lexington Avenue, with gold wallpaper and royal-blue banquettes. Chopsticks were provided in little paper sheaths, but Jane reached for the knife and fork also set beside the plates. I asked her, 'Your other dates let you get away with that?'

She blushed and bristled defensively. 'My other dates, as you call them, don't take me to Chinese restaurants that often.'

I tried not to be curious about her life in the long stretches when I wasn't there; it would have been painful for me to know too much, and painful for her to confess that there wasn't much to know. 'Not classy enough, I suppose,' I accused her, defensive in turn. Back in Buffalo, a Chinese meal out was a manageable treat for the kids or an easy way to see the boring couples Carole liked. I told Jane in a gentler voice, 'Chinese food and silver shouldn't mix. There's no big trick to it.' I unwrapped her chopsticks and took her long, freckled, loose-jointed hand in mine. She seemed faintly frightened. I saw myself for a second in the mirror of her female mind: I was a man, frightening, with big hands that could inflict a bruising blow. Of the chopsticks, I explained, 'You rest one of them here, against that finger, so the thumb holds it in place, and hold the other between these two, like a pencil. Feel the mobility? With this pinching motion you can pick up anything, from a single grain of rice to a chunk of sweet-and-sour pork.'

'I can do it!' she announced, after a while. 'This is wonderful! Oops. Damn.'

'Rice is the hardest. Sort of put them together. Chinese peasants use them like a shovel.'

'Over thirty,' she said, 'and I never thought I could manage the damn things. I'd watch other people twiddling away, and they seemed so debonair. *Thank you,* Stan.'

I accepted her thanks proudly. I doubt whether Jeffrey really got the hang of common denominators, but I want to think that to the day she dies Jane can handle chopsticks because of me.

I am losing her. The mist that arose when we first met, surrounded by glaring blue scrawls, threatens to swallow all the details. The chopsticks, the taxicabs in the depths of night, my excited impersonation of a man buying flowers for a sweetheart – what else can I remember? We must have talked, thousands of words, but of what? Our expertise was in quite different areas, and if we talked too long about our marriages, we would trip over the fact that hers was ended and mine was not. Once, when, after a longer absence than usual, I entered her, she breathed in my ear, 'He's home,' which almost unmanned me, it seemed so sad an untruth. My home was in Eggertsville, with the three children, the ensemble furniture, the Saturday-night dinner parties, the Sunday-morning men's tennis group for me and the Methodist choir for Carole. Jane's appeal was exactly that she was *not* home, that she was a splendid elsewhere.

New York City did not miss me; it did not occur to me that she might. Yet, explaining away a weepy mood – Jeffrey had a fever, she did not think she should leave him with Brenda from downstairs, so we sat together in our clothes, in the room with the view of the tops of the buttonwoods – Jane let drop, 'Yeah, but you haven't been racing downstairs every day to the mailbox hoping for a letter from Buffalo.'

Her letters to me, directed to my office at the plant, embarrassed me, as well as putting a funny look on the face of the department secretary as she delivered one, addressed in Jane's sprawling round handwriting, to my desk. The struggles of the gallery to survive, her glimpse at an opening of Robert Motherwell or some other giant, Jeffrey's progress at school – the details of her world, when I was not there, seemed meagre and unreal. The details of my own might estrange her by painting a life less lonely than hers. In Buffalo I had everything I needed for a life, except for her, my New York girl, tucked into my consciousness like a candy after dinner, like a mint on my pillow. 'I have nothing much to say,' I told her. 'Except that I adore you.'

'"Adore" implies a distance, doesn't it?' Jane had a stern face she reserved for people who came into the gallery just to loiter on a cold day. She clumsily stubbed out her cigarette, smoked down to the scarlet filter, in a fashionably rough clay ashtray on her stack of art books. She had caught Jeffrey's cold and kept clearing her throat.

'You don't want to hear,' I assured her, 'about which child of mine has had his bicycle stolen or which dog has died.'

'I don't?'

'Or how Carole had a flat tire doing the car pool, or how drunk so-and-so got at some other so-and-so's dinner party.'

'This woman you almost left Carole for – you still see her?'

'Althea Wadsworth. Sometimes, at big occasions. We all put a good face on it. Life must go on.'

'I suppose that's what it must do, yes.'

I was not comfortable with the tug of this conversation and went to the front windows, wondering if this was the last time I would ever see these treetops. To the north, there were few skyscrapers, just a low recession of streets and domestic windows. It might almost have been Buffalo, along Seneca Street.

'For this Althea person, you really put yourself out. You tried to leave Carole for her.'

It displeased me that Jane knew these women's names. I suppressed the impulse to explain that I had seen how Althea functioned as a suburban housewife and mother – that I could envision her fitting into Carole's slot. I knew all the furniture she would bring with her. Jane's furniture was impalpable – it was the city itself, the universe of anonymous lights.

'I did, and I swore I'd never try it again. It was too painful, for everybody.'

Jeffrey began to cough in the other room – a dry, delicate, only-child's cough – and Jane went into him.

I heard murmuring as she rubbed his back. She began to sing. I had never heard her sing. She had a sweet voice, reedy but true, with an unforeseeable hillbilly twang to it. 'You are my sunshine, my only sunshine,' she sang softly to Jeffrey. 'You make me happy when skies are gray.'

After a while, the boy asleep, she came back to me, and unhurriedly, moving about with the high-haunched ungainly grace of a deer, she took off her clothes. We made love on her foam-rubber sofa, with its shaky chrome legs, and afterwards we ate six toasted bagels and two half-pints of cream cheese. This may have been the last time I slept with her, but I'm not sure. We phased out gradually. The extruded-aluminum business was facing an onslaught of fresh foreign competition – from South Korea and Taiwan, after all we had done for them – and Buffalo became more involving and complicated, both at work and on the social front, and I stopped rigging trips to New York.

Althea and I had been married for close to fifteen years when I saw Jane again, in Rochester. Rochester, of all places, in the middle of winter, at one of the entrances to the down-town mall, where they have the totem pole and the clock with little puppet shows. Christmas was over, and the season's snowfalls had been compressed to a blotchy corrugated ice, hard as iron. Jane was accompanied by a blond child I took for Jeffrey; but of course Jeffrey would be in his twenties, I realized. The boy was tugging at her, against the tilt of her crooked smile, and I could hardly talk, since the old mist between us had arisen, plain as she had become. She had put on weight. Her middle-aged face was round and red beneath a wool knit cap, and she was wearing one of those black quilted winter coats that suburban matrons have taken to wearing as work uniforms. Dog hairs and what looked like a few bits of straw were clinging to it.

'Jane, my God,' I said, reeling backward from the firm, even complacent hug she bestowed, through our wraps. 'What are you doing here?'

'I live here,' she announced. 'In Irondequoit, actually. We bought an old farm.'

We? I put off exploring that. 'How – how long?'

'Oh, ten years. This is Tommy.'

'Where's Jeffrey?'

'In Taos, trying to be a painter, the poor darling. God, it's been bliss for me to get away from *art*ists. What selfish boyish shits they all are. Ken works for Kodak – he's a chemist. We met the way you and I did – he was trying to sell the gallery some process.'

'Not a process, I just wanted to look at flanges. But can you stand it, Jane, out of New York? The city, I mean.'

She put a great black-mittened hand on mine, and even through the wool-lined leather I felt the rightness of her touch, the velvety rightness come back to me, a texture of youth, when the world still bristles with options. I felt in her presence the fear of death a man feels with a woman who once opened herself to him and is available no more.

'I hated New York, I was dying to get out of it. You knew that, Stan. It's what made you shy.'

'I –'

But the strange child was tugging her toward some keenly imagined pleasure within the mall, and her hand was yanked awkwardly away. Flipping that hand in mid-air, she urged, 'Don't say a thing, sweetie. Be happy for me is all you have to do.'

Licks of Love in the Heart
of the Cold War

Khrushchev was in power, or we thought he was, that month I spent as cultural ambassador and banjo-picking bridge between the superpowers, helping stave off nuclear holocaust. It was September into October of 1964. We had a cultural-exchange program with the Soviets at the time. Our State Department's theory was that almost any American, paraded before the oppressed Soviet masses, would be, just in his easy manner of walking and talking, such an advertisement for the free way of life that cells of subversion would pop up in his wake like dandelions on an April lawn. So my mission wasn't as innocent as it seemed. Still, I was game to undertake it.

My happy home lies in western Virginia, which isn't the same as West Virginia, though it's getting close, on the far side of the Blue Ridge. Washington, D.C., to me spells Big City, and when the official franked letters began to come through it never occurred to me to resist something as big and beautiful as the pre-Vietnam U.S. government. And Russia, it's just one more mess of a free-enterprise country now, but then it was the dark side of the moon. The Aeroflot plane from Paris smelled of boiled potatoes, as I recall, and the stewardesses were as hefty as packed suitcases. When we landed at midnight we might have been descending over the ocean, there were so few lights under us.

The airport was illuminated as if by those dim bedside lamps hotels give you, not to read by. One of the young soldiers was pawing through a well-worn *Playboy* some blushing fur-trader ahead of me had tried to smuggle in, and my first impression of how life worked under Communism was the glare of that poor centerfold's sweet bare skin under those brownish airport lights. The magazine was confiscated, but I just don't want to believe the travelling salesman was sent to the gulag. He had a touch of Asia in his cheekbones – it wasn't like we had corrupted a pure-blooded Russian. The State Department boys swooped me out the customs door into a chauffeured limo that smelled not of boiled potatoes exactly but very deeply of tobacco, another natural product. My granddaddy's barn used to smell like that, even after the cured leaf had been baled and sold. I – Eddie Chester, internationally admired banjo-picker – knew I was going to like it here.

On the airport road into Moscow in those days there was this humongous billboard of Lenin, leaning forward with a wicked goateed grin and pointing to something up above with a single finger, like John the Baptist pointing to a Jesus we couldn't see yet. 'I love that,' my chief State Department escort said from the jump seat. 'To three hundred million people – "up yours."' His name was Bud Nevins, cultural attaché. I saw a lot of Bud, Bud and his lovely wife, Libby, in the weeks to come.

Already, Washington had been an adventure. I had

been briefed, a couple of afternoons, by a mix of our experts and refugees from the Soviet Union. One portly old charmer, who had been upper-middle management in the KGB, filled a whole afternoon around a long leather table telling me what restaurants to go to and what food to order. Smoked sturgeon, *pirozhki*, mushroom pie. His mouth was watering, though from the look of him he hadn't been exactly starved under capitalism. Still, no food like home cooking; I could sympathize with that. Those Washington people, they did love to party. After each briefing there would be a reception, and at one of the receptions a little black-haired coffee-fetcher from that afternoon's briefing came up to me as if her breasts were being offered on a tray. They were sizable pert breasts, in a peach-colored chemise that had just outgrown being a T-shirt.

'Sir, you are my god,' she told me. That's always nice to hear, and she shouldn't have spoiled it by adding, 'Except of course for Earl Scruggs. And that nice tall Allen Shelton, who used to fill in on banjo with the Virginia Boys; oh, he was *cute*! Now, have you heard those new sides the McReynoldses have cut down in Jacksonville, with this boy called Bobby Thompson? *He* is the future! He has this whole new style – you can hear the melody! "Hard Hearted." "Dixie Hoedown." Oh, my!'

'Young lady, you know I'm not exactly bluegrass,' I told her politely. 'Earl, well, he's beginning to miss notes, but you can't get away from him, he's a giant, all right, and Don Reno likewise. Nevertheless, my above-all admiration is Pete Seeger, if you must know.

He's the one, him and the Weavers, brought back the five-string after the war, after the dance bands had turned the banjo as cute as a ukulele.'

'He is folksy and *pokey* and phony, if you're asking me,' she said, with that hurried overemphasis I was beginning to get used to, while her warm black eyes darted back and forth around my face like stirred-up horseflies. 'And a traitor to his country besides.'

'Well,' I admitted, 'you won't find him on *Grand Ole Opry* real soon, but the college kids eat him up, and he does sheer, sincere picking – none of that show-biz flash that sometimes bothers me about old Earl. Young lady, you should calm yourself and sit down and listen sometime to those albums Pete cut with Woody and the Almanacs before the war.'

'I did,' she said eagerly. 'I did, I did. *Talking Union*. *Sod Buster Ballads*. Wonderful true-blue lefty stuff. The West Coast Communies must have loved it. Mr. Chester, did you ever in your life listen to a program called *Jamboree* out of Wheeling?'

'Did I? I got my first airtime on it, on good old WWVA. Me and Jim Buchanan on fiddle, before he got big. "Are You Lost in Sin?" and "Don't Say Good-bye If You Love Me," with a little "Somebody Loves You, Darlin'" for a rideout. Did I catch your name, may I ask?'

'You'll laugh. It's a silly name.'

'I bet, now, it isn't. You got to love the name the good Lord gave you.'

'It wasn't the good Lord, it was my hateful mother,' she said, and, taking a deep breath that rounded out her

cheeks like a trumpet player's, came out with 'Imogene.'
Then she exhaled in a blubbery rush and asked me,
'Imogene Frye. Isn't it silly like I said?'

'No,' I said. It was my first lie to her. She seemed a
little off-center, right from the first, but Imogene could
talk banjo, and here in this city of block-long buildings
and charcoal suits that was as welcome to me as borscht
and salted cucumbers would would have been to that
homeless KGB colonel, locked out forever as a traitor
from the land he loved.

'I *loved*,' this Imogene was saying, 'the licks you took
on "Heavy Traffic Ahead." And the repeat an octave
higher on "Walking in Jerusalem Just Like John."'

'It wasn't an octave, it was a fifth,' I told her, settling
in and lifting two bourbons from a silver tray a kindly
Negro was carrying around. I saw that this was going
to be a conversation. Banjos were getting to be hot
then, what with that *Beverly Hillbillies* theme, and
I didn't want to engage with any shallow groupie.
'Do you ever tune in,' I asked her, 'WDBJ, out of
Roanoke? And tell me exactly why you think this
Bobby Thompson is the future.'

She saw my hurt, with those hot bright eyes that
looked to be all pupil, and hastened to reassure me in
her hurried, twitchy way of talking that I was the
present, the past, and the future as far as she was
concerned. Neither of us, I think, had the habit of
drinking, but the trays kept coming around, brought
by black men in white gloves, and by the time the
reception was breaking up the whole scene might have
been a picture printed on silk, waving gently in and

out. The Iron Curtain experts had drifted away to their homes in Bethesda and Silver Springs, and it seemed the most natural thing in the free world that little Imogene, to whom I must have looked a little wavy myself, would be inviting me back to her apartment somewhere off in one of those neighborhoods where they say it's not safe for a white man to show his face late at night.

Black and white, that's most of what I remember. Her hair was black and soft, and her skin was white and soft, and her voice had slowed and gotten girlish with the effects of liquor and being romanced. I was on the floor peeling down her pantyhose while she rested a hand on the top of my head for balance. Then we were sitting on the bed while she cupped her hands under those sizable breasts, pointing them at me like guns. 'I want them to be even bigger,' she told me so softly I strained to hear, 'for *you*.' Her breasts being smooched made her smile in the slanted streetlight like a round-faced cartoon character, a cat-and-canary smile. When I carried the courtesies down below, this seemed to startle her, so she stiffened a bit before relaxing her legs and letting them spread. The men she had known before didn't do this, back then before Vietnam took away our innocence, but ever since my days of car-seat courtship I've liked to press my face into a girlfriend's nether soul, to taste the waters in which we all must swim out to the light. I strove to keep my manly focus amid the jiggling caused by government-issue alcohol, my wondering what time it was, the jostling of my conscience, and the distractions of this environment, with its sadness of the single girl. Black and white – her little room was sucked dry of color like something on early TV, her bureau with its brushes and silver-framed photos of the family that had hatched her, an armchair with a cellophane-wrapped drugstore-rental book still balanced on one arm, where she had left it before heading off this morning into her working day, her FM/AM/shortwave portable radio big enough to pick up stations from Antarctica, her narrow bed with its brass headboard that was no good to lean on when we had done our best and needed to reminisce and establish limits.

'Lordy,' I said. This was something of a lie, since when the main event came up I had lost a certain energy to the good times behind us, beginning hours ago at the party. I had felt lost in her.

She touched my shoulder and said my full name tentatively, as if I wouldn't like it. 'Eddie Chester.' She was right; it sounded proprietorial and something in me bristled. 'You really are a god.'

'You should catch me sober sometime.'

'When?' Her voice pounced, quick and eager like it had been at first. The pieces of white beside her swollen pupils glinted like sparkles on TV. Her propped-up pillow eclipsed half her face and half a head of black hair mussed out to a wild size.

Mine had just been a manner of speaking. 'Not ever, it may be, Imogene,' I told her. 'I have a week of gigs out west, and then I'm off on this trip, helping keep your planet safe for democracy.'

'But I'll see you when you come back,' she insisted. 'You must come back to Washington, to be debriefed. Eddie, Eddie, Eddie,' she said, as if knowing repetition galled me. 'I can't ever let you go.'

Imogene's magic essences had dried on my face and I longed for a washcloth and a taxi out of there. 'I got a wife, you know. And three little ones.'

'Do you love your wife?'

'Well, honey, I wouldn't say I don't, though after fifteen years a little of the bloom rubs off.'

'Do you kiss her between the legs, too?'

This did seem downright forward. 'I forget,' I said, and pushed out of the bed into the bathroom, where the switch brought back color into everything, all those pinks and blues and yellows on her medicine-cabinet shelves; it seemed she needed a lot of pills to keep herself functional.

'Eddie, don't go,' she pleaded. 'Stay the night. It's not safe out there. It's so bad the taxis won't come even if you call.'

'Young lady, I got a hired car coming to the Willard Hotel at seven-thirty tomorrow morning to carry me back to western Virginia, and I'm going to be there. I may not be the future of banjo-picking, but I take a real professional pride in never having missed a date.' Putting on my underwear, I remembered how the taxi had gone around past the railroad station and then the Capitol, all lit up, and I figured we hadn't gone so far past it I couldn't steer myself by its tip, or by the spotlights on the Washington Monument.

'Eddie, you *can't* go, I won't let you,' Imogene

asserted, out of bed, all but one sweet fat white leg caught in the sheet. Her breasts didn't look quite so cocky without her holding them up for me. That's the trouble with a full figure, it ties you to a bra.

I crooned a few lines of 'Don't Say Good-bye If You Love Me,' until my memory ran out, though I could see Jim Buchanan's face inches across from me, squeezed into its fiddle, at the WWVA microphone. And then I told Imogene, as if still quoting a lyric, 'Little darlin', you ain't keeping me here, though I must say it was absolute bliss.' This was my third lie, but a white one, and with some truth still in it. 'Now, you go save your undying affection for an unattached man.'

'You'll be killed!' she shrieked, and clawed at me for a while, but I shushed and sweet-talked her back into her bed, fighting a rising headache all the while, and let myself out into the stairwell. The street, one of those numbered ones, was as still as a stage set, but, stepping out firmly in my cowboy boots, I headed toward what I figured was west – you get a sense of direction, growing up in the morning shadow of the Blue Ridge – and, sure enough, I soon caught a peek of the Capitol dome in the distance, white as an egg in an eggcup. A couple of tattered colored gentlemen stumbled toward me from a boarded-up doorway, but I gave them both a dollar and a hearty God bless and strode on. If a man can't walk around in his own country without fear, what business has he selling freedom to the Russians?

*

Bud Nevins got me and my banjos – a fine old Gibson mother-of-pearl-trimmed Mastertone and an S. S. Stewart backup whose thumb string always sounded a little punky – into Moscow and put us all to bed in a spare room of the big apartment he and Libby and three children occupied in the cement warehouse where the Russians stashed free-world diplomatic staff. Mrs. Nevins was a long-haired strawberry blonde beginning to acquire that tight, worried expression the wives of professors and government officials get, from being saddled with their husbands' careers. You get the pecking-order blues. The bygone Soviet summer hadn't done much to refresh her freckles, and a long white winter lay ahead. This was late September, shirt-less apple-picking time back home. The bed they put me in, the puff smelled old-fashionedly of flake soap, the way my mother's laundry used to when I'd help her carry the wicker basket heavy with wet wash out to the clothesline. Ma and I were never closer than around wet wash.

As he put me to bed Nevins said there was some-thing already come for me in the diplomatic pouch. An envelope lay on my pillow, addressed to me care of the embassy APO number in a scrunched-up hand in black ballpoint. Inside was a long letter from Imogene, recounting her sorrowful feelings after I left, guessing I was still alive because my death in her neighborhood hadn't been in the papers and she had caught on the radio a plug for an appearance of mine in St. Louis. She recalled some sexual details I wasn't sure needed to be set down on paper, and promised undying love.

I just skimmed the second page. Her words weren't easy to read, like the individual letters wanted to double back on themselves, and I was dog-tired from those thousands of miles I had travelled to reach the dark side of the moon.

Now, I've seen a lot of friendly crowds in the course of my professional life, but I must say I've never seen so many lovable, well-disposed people as I did that month in Russia. They were, at least the ones that weren't in any gulag, full of beans – up all night and bouncy the next morning. The young ones didn't have that shadowy look American children were taking on in those years, as if dragged outdoors from watching television; these young Russians seemed to be looking directly at life in its sunshine and its hazard. I was sorry to think it, but they were unspoiled. Grins poured from the students I would play for, in one drafty old classroom after another. Converted ballrooms, many of them seemed to be, or not even converted – they just hauled the czarist dancers and musicians out and moved the Communist desks in. There were dusty moldings and plaster garlands high along the peeling plaster walls, with the walls still painted pastel ballroom colors, and plush drapes rotting around the view of some little damp park where old ladies in babushkas, so gnarled and hunched our own society would have had them on the junk heap, were sweeping the dirt paths with brooms that were just twigs wrapped around a stick. You used what you had here. People had so little material goods they had to take pleasure just in being alive.

I had worked up a little talk, allowing time for the translation. I would begin with the banjo as an African instrument, called *banza* in the French West African colonies and *banjer* in the American South, where in some backwaters you could still hear it called that. Slaves played it, and then there were the travelling minstrel shows, where white performers like Dan Emmett and Joel Walker Sweeney still used the traditional black 'stroke' or 'frailing' or 'claw-hammer' style of striking down across the strings with thumb and the back of the index-finger nail (I would demonstrate). Then (still demonstrating) I would tell of the rise of the 'finger-picking' or 'guitar' style, adding the middle finger and pulling *up* on the strings with metal picks added to those three nails, and ending with bluegrass and traditional folk as revived by my hero Seeger. When I had said all that in about half an hour, with samples of what we think minstrel banjo sounded like and some rags from the 1890s the way Vess L. Ossman and Fred Van Eps left them on Edison cylinders and ending with a little Leadbelly, they would ask me why Americans oppressed our black people.

I got better at answering that one, as I strummed and picked and rolled through those echoing classrooms. I stopped saying that slavery had been universal not long ago and the Russians had had their serfs, that several hundred thousand white men from the North had died so that slaves could be free, that a hundred years later civil-rights laws had been passed and lynching had become a rarity. I could tell, as I stood there listening to myself being translated, that I was losing them, it was too much like what they heard from their own teachers, too much pie in the sky. I changed to saying simply yes, it was a problem, a disgraceful problem, but that I honestly believed that America was working at it, and music was one of the foremost ways it was working at it. Listening to myself talk, I'd sometimes think the State Department knew what it was doing, bringing a natural patriotic optimist like me over here. Ever since JFK had got shot, my breed was harder to find. They must have had a pretty fat file on me somewhere: the thought made me uneasy.

It felt best when I played, played as if for a country-fair crowd back home, and those young Russian faces would light up as if I were telling jokes. They had all heard jazz, and even some Twist and early rock on tapes that were smuggled through, but rarely anything so jaunty and tinny and jolly, so *irrepressible*, as banjo music going full steam, when your fingers do the thinking and you listen in amazement yourself. Sometimes they would pair me with a balalaika player, and one little Azerbaijani, I think he had some Gypsy blood, tried my instrument, and I his. We made an act of it for a few days, touring the Caucasus, hill towns where old men with beards would gather outside the auditorium windows as if sipping moonshine. When they had advertised ahead for a formal concert, the crowds were so big the Soviet controllers cut down on the schedule.

The translator who travelled with me varied but usually it was Nadia, a lean thin-lipped lady over forty who had learned her English during the war, in the military. She had lost two brothers and a fiancé to Herr Hitler, and was wed to the Red system with bonds of iron and grief. She looked like a skinny tall soldier boy herself, just out of uniform – no lipstick, long white waxy nose, and a feathery short haircut with gray coming in not in strands but in patches. Blank-faced, she would listen to me spiel, give a nod when she'd heard all she could hold, and spout out a stream of this language that was, with all its mushy twisty sounds, pure music to me. The more she and I travelled together, the better she knew what I was going to say, and the longer she could let me go before translating, and the more I could hear individual words go by, little transparent phrases through which I seemed to see into her like into the windows of a town as your train whips through. We travelled on trains in the same compartment, so I could look down from the top bunk and see her hands remove her shoes and her mustard-colored stockings from her feet. Then her bare feet and hands would flitter out of sight. I would listen, but never hear her breathing relax; she confessed to me, toward the end of my stay, that she could never sleep on trains. The motion and the clicking stirred her up.

An inhibiting factor was Bud Nevins being in the compartment with us – there were two bunks on two sides – and if not Bud, another escort from our embassy, and often a fourth, an underling of Bud's or a second escort from the Soviet side, who spoke Armenian or Kazakh or whatever the language was going to be when we disembarked. Sometimes I had more escorts than would fit into one compartment; and

I expect I often got the best night's sleep, with every-body watching everybody else. Nadia was as loyal a comrade as they made them but seemed to need watch-ing anyway. As I got to know her body language I could tell when we were being crowded, politically speaking.

After a while my tendency became to bond with the Communists. When we arrived at one of our hinter-land destinations, Nadia and her associates would bundle me into a Zil and then we would share a humor-ous irritation at being tailed by an embassy watchdog in his imported Chevrolet. When we all went south, Bud came along with that willowy strawberry blonde of his. Libby had, along with her worried look, a plump pretty mouth a little too full of teeth. For all their three children, they hadn't been married ten years. Out of wifely love and loyalty she wanted to join in what fun the Soviet Union in its sinister vast size offered.

Somewhere in backwoods Georgia – their Georgia, even hillier than ours – we visited a monastery, a show-piece of religious tolerance. The skeleton crew of monks glided around with us in their grim stone rooms. The place had that depressing stuffy holy smell, old candle wax and chrism and furniture polish, I had last sniffed thirty years ago, in the storage closet of a Baptist basement Sunday school. Among the monks with beards down to their bellies was a young one, and I wondered how he had enlisted himself in this ghostly brotherhood. Demented or a government employee, I decided. He had silky long hair, like a princess captive in a tower, and the sliding bloodshot eyeballs of a spy.

He was one kind of human animal, and I was another, and when we looked at each other we each repressed a shudder.

Outside, a little crowd of shepherds and sheep, neither group looking any too clean, had gathered around the automobiles, and when Nadia made our identities and friendly mission clear to them, the shepherds invited us to dine with them, on one of the sheep. I would have settled for some cabbage soup and blini back at the Tblisi hotel, but the Nevinses looked stricken, as though this chance at authentic ethnicity and bridge-building would never come again, and I suppose it wouldn't have. Their duty was to see that I did my duty, and my duty was clear: consort with the shepherds, scoring points for the free world. I looked toward Nadia and with one of her unsmiling nods she approved, though this hadn't been on her schedule. Or, who knows, maybe it had been. By now I saw her as an ally in my mission to subvert the rule of the proletariat, no doubt deluding myself.

We climbed what seemed like a mile at least and sat down around a kind of campfire, where an ominous big kettle was mulling over some bony chunks of a creature recently as alive as we. The shepherds loved Libby's long ironed hair and the way her round freckled knees peeped out of her modified miniskirt as we squatted in our circle of rock perches. A goatskin of red wine was produced; as stated before, I'm no connoisseur of alcoholic beverages, but this stuff was so rough that flies kept dying in our cups, and a full swig took the paint off the roof of your mouth. After the goatskin had been passed a few times, Libby began to relish the shepherds' attention, to glow and giggle and switch her long limbs around and come up with her phrases of language-school Russian. Those shepherds – agricultural workers and livestock supervisors was probably how they thought of themselves – had a number of unsolved dental problems, as we saw when their whiskers cracked open in a laugh, but there was a lot of love around that simmering pot, a lot of desire for international peace. Even Bud took off his jacket and unbuttoned his top shirt button, and Nadia began to lounge back in the scree and translate me loosely, with what I heard as her own original material. The lamb when it was served, in tin bowls, could have been mulled somewhat longer and was mixed in with what looked like crabgrass, roots and all, and some little green capers that each had a firecracker inside, but as it turned out only the Nevinses got sick. Next day they had to stay in their hotel room with the shades lowered while the Communists and I motored out to entertain a People's War veterans home that had a good view of Mt. Elbrus. The way we all cackled in the car at the expense of the Nevinses and their tender capitalist stomachs was the cruellest thing I saw come to pass in my month in the Soviet Union.

Uzbekistan, Tajikistan, Kazakhstan: you wondered why the Lord ever made so much wasteland in the world, with a gold dome or blue lake now and then as a sop to the thirsty soul. But here's where the next revolution was coming from, it turned out – out from under those Islamic turbans. When my banjo flashed mother-of-pearl their way, they made the split-finger sign to warn off the evil eye. They knew a devil's gadget when they saw it.

Whenever I showed up back in Moscow I got solemnly handed packets of letters in Imogene's cramped black hand, pages and pages and pages of them. I couldn't believe the paper she would waste, as well as the abuse of taxpayer money involved in using the diplomatic pouch. She had heard me take an eight-bar vocal break on my Decca cut of 'Somebody Loves You, Darling,' on the station out of Charlottesville, and decided it was a code to announce that I was leaving my wife for her. 'I am altogether open and YOURS, my dearest DEAREST Eddie,' she wrote, if I can remember one sentence in all that trash. 'I will wait for as LONG as it takes, though KINGDOM COME in the meantime,' if I can recall another. Then on and on, with every detail of what she did each day, with some about her internal workings that I would rather not be told, though I was happy she had her period, and all about her unhappiness (that I wasn't there with her) and hopefulness (that I soon would be), and her theory that I was in the air talking to her all the time, broadcasting from every frequency on the dial, including the shortwave that brought in stations from the Caribbean and the Azores. If she caught the Osborne Brothers doing 'My Lonely Heart' and 'You'll Never Be the Same,' she knew that I was their personal friend and had asked them to send her the private message, never mind they recorded it in the early

Fifties. I couldn't do more than skim a page here and there – the handwriting got smaller and scrunchier and then would blossom out into some declaration of love printed in capitals and triple underlined. Just the envelopes, the bulky white tumble of them, were embarrassing me in front of Bud Nevins and the whole embassy staff, embattled here in the heartland of godless Communism. How could I be a cultural ambassador while shouldering this ridiculous load of arrested adolescence?

Imogene was planning where we would live, how she would dress in her seat of honor at my concerts, what she would do for me in the bedroom and the kitchen to keep my love at its present sky-high pitch. Thinking we were in for a lifetime together, she filled me in on her family, her mother that she had maligned but who wasn't all bad, and her father who was scarcely in her life enough to mention, and her brothers and sisters that sounded like the worst pack of losers and freeloaders on the DelMarVa Peninsula. Her outpourings would catch, my fear was, the vigilance of the KGB, X-raying right through the diplomatic pouch. I would lose face with Nadia, that steel-true exemplar of doing without. Those innocent-eyed gymnasium students would sense my contamination. The homely austerity of Soviet life, with that undercurrent of fear still humming from Stalin, made the amorous self-delusions of this childish American woman repulsive to me. As my month approached its end, and the capitalist world put out feelers to reclaim me, Imogene's crazy stuff got mixed in with business cables from my

agency and colorless but loving letters from my wife
with enclosed notes and dutiful drawings from my
children: this heightened my disgust. I would have
sent a cable – CUT IT OUT, or YOU AIN'T NO BLUE-
EYED SWEETHEART OF MINE – but by some canniness
of her warped mind she never gave a return address,
and when I tried to think of her apartment all I got
was that black-and-white feeling, the way she fed me
her breasts one at a time, the very big radio, and the
empty street with the Capitol at the end like a white-
chocolate candy. I had simply to endure it, this sore
humiliation.

They had saved Leningrad for me to the last, since it
was where the Communists, still remembering the
Siege, were the toughest, and I might run into the
most hostility from an audience. But as soon as my
Gibson began talking, the picked strings all rolling like
the synchronized wheels, big and little, of the Wabash
Cannonball, the smiles of mutual understanding would
start breaking out. I am not a brave man, but I have
faith in my instrument and in people's basic decent
instincts. St. Petersburg, as we call it again, is one
beautiful city, a Venice where you least expect it, all
those big curved buildings in Italian colors. The students in their gloomy old ballrooms were worried about
Goldwater getting elected, and I told them the American people would never elect a warmonger. I was always
introduced as a 'progressive' American folk artist, but
I had to tell them that there wasn't much progressive
about me: my folks had been lifelong Democrats

because of a war fought a hundred years ago, and I wasn't going to be the one to change parties.

Then, just as I was about to get back onto Aeroflot, Khrushchev was pushed out of power, and all the Soviets around me tightened up, wary of what was going to happen next. This whole huge empire, think of it, run out of some vodka-soaked back rooms by a few beetle-browed men. Nadia – my voice, my guide, my protector, closer to me for this month than a wife, because I couldn't have done without her – complimented me by confiding, somewhere out on the Nevskii Prospekt or in some hallway where no bugs were not likely to be placed, 'Eddie, it was not civilized. It was not done how a civilized country should do things. We should have said to him, "Thank you very much for ending the terror." And then, "You are excused – too much adventurism, O.K., failures in agricultural production, and et cetera. O.K., so long, but *bolshoi* thanks."'

There would be a moment, toward the end of a long public day in, say, Tashkent, when her English would deteriorate, just sheer weariness from drawing upon a double set of brain cells, and her eyelids and the tip of her long white nose would get pink. We would say good night in the hotel lobby, with its musty attic smell and lamps whose bases were brass bears, and she would give me in her handshake not the palm and meat of the thumb but four cool fingers, aligned like a sergeant's stripes. And that was the way we began to say goodbye in the airport, until we leaped the gulf between our two great countries and I kissed her on one cheek and then the other and hugged her, in proper Slavic style. Her eyes teared up, but it may have been just the start of a cold.

Bud told me in the airport, so casually I should have smelled trouble, 'We took you off the APO number two days ago, so your mail won't show up here after you leave. It will be forwarded to your home.'

'Sounds reasonable,' I said, not thinking it through. I suspect Bud foresaw the complications, but he was a diplomat, a pro at saying no more than required.

Coming back, the last leg, out of Paris, I had an experience such as I've never had in all my miles of flying. We came down on the big arc over Gander and Nova Scotia and, five miles up, I could see New York from hundreds of miles away, a little blur of light in the cold plastic oval of the plane window. It grew and grew, like a fish I was pulling in. My cheek got cold against the plastic as I pressed to keep it in view, a little spot on the invisible surface of the earth like a nebula, like a dust mouse, only glowing, the fuzzy center of our American dream. Just it and me, there in the night sky, communing. It was a vision.

After I cleared customs at what had been Idlewild until recently, I phoned home. It was after ten o'clock, but I was powerfully glad to be again in the land of the free. My wife answered with something else in her voice besides welcome, like a fearful salamander under a flat rock. 'Some letters for you came today and yesterday,' she said. 'All from one person, it looks like.'

How bright, I was thinking, this place was, compared to the Moscow airport. Every corner and rampway was lit as harsh as a mug shot, the whole place packed with advertisements and snack bars and sizzling with electricity. 'Did you open them?' I asked, my heart suddenly plunked by a heavy hand.

'Just one,' she said. 'That was enough, Eddie. Oh, my.'

'It wasn't anything,' I began, which wasn't a hundred percent true. For, though in one part of me I was not happy with Imogene for making what looked to be an ongoing talking point in my little family, on the other hand you can't blame a person too hard for thinking you're a god. You have to feel a spark of fondness, remembering the way she held up one breast and then the other, each nipple looking in that black-and-white room like the hole of a gun barrel pointed straight at your mouth. You can go to the dark side of the moon and back and see nothing more wonderful and strange than the way men and women manage to get together.

The Women Who Got Away

Pierce Junction was an isolated New Hampshire town somewhat dignified by the presence of a small liberal-arts college; we survived by clustering together like a ball of snakes in a desert cave. The Sixties had taught us the high moral value of copulation, and we were slow to give up on an activity so simultaneously pleasurable and healthy. Still, you couldn't sleep with everybody: we were bourgeoisie, responsible, with jobs and children, and affairs demanded energy and extracted wear and tear. We hadn't learned yet to take the emotion out of sex. Looking back, the numbers don't add up to what an average college student now manages in four years. There were women you failed ever to sleep with; these, in retrospect, have a perverse vividness, perhaps because the contacts, in the slithering ball of snakes, were so few that they have stayed distinct.

'Well, Martin,' Audrey Lancaster murmured to me toward the end of a summer cruise on a boat hired out of Portsmouth in celebration of somebody or other's fortieth birthday, 'I see what they say about you, at last.' The 'at last' was a dig of sorts, and the 'they' was presumably female in gender. I wondered how much conversation went on, and along lines how specific, among the wives and divorcées of our set. I had been standing there by the rail, momentarily alone, mellow on my portion of California Chablis, watching the Piscataqua River shakily reflect the harbor lights as the boat swung to dock and the loudspeaker system piped Simon and Garfunkel into the warm, watery night.

My wife was slow-dancing on the forward deck with her lover, Frank Greer. Audrey had materialized beside me and my hand went around her waist as if we might dance, too. There my hand stayed, and, like the gentle buzz you get from a frayed appliance cord, the reality of her haunch burned through to my fingers and palm. She was a solid, smooth-faced woman, so nearsighted that she moved with a splay-footed pugnacity, as if something she didn't quite see might knock her over. Her contact lenses were always getting lost, in somebody's lawn or at the back of her eyeballs. She had married young and was a bit younger than the rest of us. You had to love Audrey, seeing her out on the tennis court in frayed denim cut-offs, with her sturdy brown legs and big, squinty smile, missing the ball completely. Her waist was smooth and flexible in summer cotton, and, yes, she was right, for the first time in all our years of acquaintance I sensed her as a potential mate, as a piece of the cosmic puzzle that might fit my piece.

But I also felt that, basically, she didn't care for me, not enough to come walking through all of adultery's risks and spasms of guilt, all those hoops of flame. She distrusted me, the way you distrust a competitor. We were both clowns, bucking to be elected Funniest in the Class. Further, she was taken, doubly: not only

married, to a man called Spike, with the four children
customary for our generation, but involved in a number
of murky flirtations or infatuations, including one with
my best friend, Rodney Miller – if a person could be
said to have same-sex friends in our rather doctrinairely
heterosexual enclave. She had a nice way of drawling
out poisonous remarks, and said now, to me, 'Shouldn't
you go tell Jeanne and Frank the boat is about to dock?
They might get arrested by the Portsmouth fuzz for
public indecency.'

I said, 'Why me? I'm not the cruise director.'

Jeanne was my wife. Her love for Frank, in the
twisted way of things back then, helped bind me to
her: I felt so sorry for her, having to spend most of her
hours with me and the children when her heart was
elsewhere. She had been raised a French Catholic, and
there was something noble for her about suffering and
self-denial; her invisible hairshirt kept her torso erect
as a dancer's and added to her beauty in my eyes. I
didn't like Audrey mocking her. Or did I? Perhaps my
feelings were more primitive, more stupidly possessive,
than I knew at the time. I tightened my grip on
Audrey's waist, approaching a painful pinch, then let
go, and went forward to where Jeanne and Frank,
the music stopped, looked as if they had just woken
up, with bloated, startled faces. Frank Greer had
been married, to a wife named Winifred, until rather
recently in our little local history. Divorce, which had
been flickering at our edges for a decade while our vast
pool of children slowly bubbled up through the school
grades toward, we hoped, psychological sturdiness, was

still rare, and sat raw on Frank, like the red cheek he had been pressing against my wife's as if against a sweaty pillow.

Maureen Miller, in one of those intervals in bed when passion had been slaked but an awkward half-hour of usable time remained before I could in decency sneak away, once told me that Winifred resented the fact that, in the years when the affair between Frank and Jeanne was common knowledge, I had never made a pass at her. Winifred, sometimes called Freddy, was an owlish small woman, a graceful white owl, with big dark eyes and untanned skin and an Emily Dickinson hairdo atop a plump body that tapered to small and shapely hands and feet. If my wife held herself like a dancer, it was her lover's wife who in fact could dance, with a feathery nestling and lightness of fit that had an embarrassing erotic effect on me. Holding her in my arms, I would get an erection, and thus I would prudently avoid dancing with her until the end of the evening, when one or the other of us, in an attempt to persuade our spouses to tear themselves apart, would have put on an overcoat. Otherwise, I was not attracted to Winifred. Like the model for her hairdo, she had literary ambitions and a dogmatic, clipped, willfully oblique style. She seemed in her utterances faintly too firm.

'Well, I won't say no,' she said, not altogether graciously, one night well after midnight when Jeanne suggested that I walk Winifred home, through a snow-storm that had developed during a dinner party of ours and its inert, boozy aftermath. Couples or their remnants had drifted off until just Winifred was left; she had a stern, impassive way of absorbing a great deal of liquor and betraying its presence in her system only by a slight lowering of her lids over her bright black eyes, and an increase of pedantry in her fluting voice. This was before the Greers' divorce. Frank was absent from the party on some mysterious excuse of a business trip. It was the first stage of their separation, I realized later. Jeanne, knowing more than she let on, had extended herself that night like a kid sister to the unescorted woman. She kept urging Freddy, as the party thinned, to give us one more tale of the creative-writing seminar she was taking, as a special student, at our local college, Bradbury. Bradbury had formerly been a bleak little Presbyterian seminary tucked up here, with its pillared chapel, in the foothills of the White Mountains, but it had long loosened its ecclesiastical ties and in the Sixties had gone coed, with riotous results.

'This one girl,' Winifred said, accepting what she swore was her last Kahlúa and brandy, 'read a story that must have been *very* closely based on a painful breakup she had just gone through, and got nothing but the *most* sarcastic comments from the instructor, who seems to be a real sadist, or else it was his way of putting the make on her.' Her expression conveyed disgust and weariness with all such transactions. I supposed that she was displacing her anger at Frank onto the instructor, a New York poet who no doubt wished he was back in Greenwich Village, where the sexual revolution was polymorphous. He was a dreary sour condescending fellow, in my occasional brushes with him, and disconcertingly short as well.

These rehashed class sessions were all fascinating stuff, if you judged from Jeanne's animation and gleeful encouragement of the other woman to tell more. A rule of life in Pierce Junction demanded that you be especially nice to your lover's spouse – by no means an insincere observance, for the secret sharing did breed a tortuous, guilt-warmed gratitude to the everyday keeper of such a treasure. But even Winifred through her veils of Kahlúa began to feel uncomfortable, and stood up in our cold room (the thermostat had retired hours ago), and put her shawl up around her head, as if flufffing up her feathers. She accepted with a frown Jeanne's insistent suggestion that I escort her home. 'Of course I'm in no condition to drive, this has been *so* lovely,' she said to Jeanne, with a handshake that Jeanne turned into a fierce, pink-faced, rather frantic (I thought) embrace of transposed affection.

Winifred's car had been plowed fast to the curb by the passing revolving-eyed behemoths of our town highway department, and she lived only three blocks away, an uphill slog in four inches of fresh snow. She did seem to need to take my arm, but we both stayed wrapped in our own thoughts. The snow drifted down with a steady whisper of its own, and the presence on the streets, at this profoundly nocturnal hour, of the churning, scraping snowplows made an effect of companionship – of a wider party beneath the low sky, which was glowing yellow with that strange, secretive phosphorescence of a snowstorm. The houses were dark, and my porch light grew smaller, receding down the hill. In front of her own door, right under a street-lamp, Winifred turned to face me as if, in our muffling clothes, to dance; but it was only to offer up her pale, oval, rather frozen and grieving face for me to kiss; snowflakes were caught in the long lashes of her closed lids and spangled the arc of parted dark hair left exposed by her shawl. I felt the usual arousal. The house behind her held only sleeping children. Its clapboard face, needing a coat of paint, looked shabby, betraying the distracted marriage within.

There was, in Pierce Junction, a romance of other couples' houses – the merged tastes, the accumulated furniture, the framed photographs going back to the bridal day and the premarital vacation spots. We loved being guests and hosts both, but preferred being guests, invasive and inquisitive and irresponsible. Did she expect me to come in? It didn't strike me as at all a feasible idea – at my back, down the hill, Jeanne would be busy tidying up the party wreckage in our living room and resting a despairing eye on the kitchen clock with its sweeping red second hand. Tiny stars of ice clotted my own lashes as I kissed our guest good night, square on the mouth but lightly, lightly, with liquor-glazed subtleties of courteous regret. Of all the kisses I gave and received in Pierce Junction, from children and adults and golden retrievers, that chaste crystalline one has remained unmelted in my mind.

When I returned to the house, Frank, surprisingly, was sitting in the living room, holding a beer and wearing a rumpled suit, his long face pink as if after great exertion. Jeanne, too tired to be flustered, explained, 'Frank just got back from his trip. The plane into the Manchester airport almost didn't land, and when he found Freddy not at their home he thought he'd swing down here and pick her up.'

'Up and down that hill in this blizzard?' I marvelled. I didn't remember any car going by.

'We have four-wheel drive,' Frank said, as if that explained everything.

Maureen could be a raucous tease. Her rangy body was wide but not deep – she had broad hips but shallow breasts – and all summer she bore around the base of her neck a pink noose of sunburn, freckled and flaking, from working in her garden in a peasant blouse and no sunhat. A redhead, she remained loyal to the long, ironed hair of the flower-child era years after the flower children had gone underground or crazy or back to their parents. When I described these events to her, leaving out the odd physiological effect which holding Winifred in my arms always produced, Maureen laughed and tossed her mane as if about to devour me with her prominent white teeth. 'Jeanne is incredible,' she said. 'Imagine setting a date with your boyfriend at one in the morning in the faith that your husband would be off sleeping with the guy's wife! It sounds as though the snowstorm held everything up – that's why she kept egging Freddy to stay.'

'I can't believe,' I said, as primly as I could while wearing no clothes, propped up in her bed with a cigarette and a glass of dark vermouth, 'that things are

65

as cold-blooded and as, as *set-up* as that. My guess is he swung by because he thought the party was still on.'

'But he could see there weren't any cars!'

'Ah,' I said, in modest triumph, 'Freddy's car *was* out front, plowed in.'

'Plowing, that's the theme,' Maureen said. ' "If ye had not plowed with my heifer" – what? – "ye had not found out my riddle." ' She and Rodney had met at a summer Bible school, and Rodney still retained the well-combed, boyish shine of a future missionary. 'Anyway,' she went on gaily, giving the bed such a bounce that I spilled vermouth into the hairs of my chest, where – damn! – Jeanne might smell it, 'I can see you feel you let Freddy down, but don't. She's screwing that odious little New York poet, everybody at Bradbury says.'

'I wish you wouldn't tell me all this. I'd like to keep some innocence.'

'Martin, you *love* it, you love knowing *every*thing,' she told me, and nuzzled at the spilled vermouth with a faceless, thrusting, leonine seriousness that rather frightened me. I fought her off by finding her ears in all that hair and using them as handles to pull her head up from my chest. Her face, thus tugged back, with uplifted upper lip and slit eyes, reminded me of Winifred's held to be kissed in the snow, and of a death mask. Maureen's was not a female body that hid its bones, its lean doomed hunger. Laughing but hard-eyed, spiteful though playful, she said, 'Rodney says you're just like a woman, you're so nosy.'

This hurt me and aroused me. Rodney and I were

severely discreet, talking about nothing but our chaste sports – golf, poker, tennis, skiing. We didn't even talk politics, at the height of Vietnam and then through Nixon's prolonged downfall. Yet it was stirring, to think of Maureen and Rodney talking about me, in their marital intimacy. 'Like a woman, am I?' I said, growling and wrestling her under, to reverse our positions in the bed, that guest-room bed I knew so well, a mahogany four-poster, with a removable pineapple topping each post. Maureen's shrieks of resistance and amusement rang through the oak-floored rooms of her Victorian house and out, I feared, into the street.

Pierce Junction was a town of secrets that kept leaking out, like sawdust from a termite-ridden beam. There were all these tiny wormholes, with a flicker of life at the end of each. When Jeanne learned of my affair with Maureen, she reacted with a surge of fury that surprised me, since I had been putting up with her and Frank for years. Unforgivably, she demonstrated her anger by storming over to the Millers' and telling Rodney everything. Maureen, with her pious streak, worked Wednesdays and Saturdays at a Methodist home for delinquent children in Concord, and it was the telephone company's efficiency, listing non-local calls by town and number, that had given our liaison away. When I try to recall our passion, it comes not with X-rated images from our hours in bed but with a certain dull taste, the madeleine of an especially desolate minute in an idle day, the longing that made me, of a dull and hollow afternoon, insatiably crave the sound of her voice – lower and huskier over the phone, more thoughtfully musical, than it seemed when we were face to face. Her voice momentarily pushed aside the sore dread in which I lived in those years; her voice, and its quick inspirations of caustic perception, painted the world, which seemed to me rimmed with a vague terror, in bright fearless colors. Hearing Maureen reassuringly laugh, as if we were all caught in a delicious, precarious joke, slaked a thirst that weighed in my throat like an iron bar. Without her in it somewhere, at least as a voice over the telephone, the world lacked a center. I *had* to talk to her, though the phone bill did us in.

The hunger was not only mine, but pervaded our circle with the pathos of unsatisfied need: poor Jeanne and Frank, stealing that silly half-hour in the blizzard. Maureen for me was a campfire whose light made the encircling darkness seem absolute, and whose heat became a sharp chill a few paces from its immediate vicinity.

Jeanne didn't come back from her interview with Rodney for hours. Not immediately, but after some days had worn us down to skeletons of weary honesty, she confessed that, Maureen being absent, she had slept with him, in some delirium of revenge, though he had been reluctant.

'One of Maureen's sadnesses,' I told her, 'was always that he was so faithful, so satisfied by her. Or so she thought.'

'How funny of her. You remember that period when Winifred and Frank were just breaking up, and Freddy was wildly on the make? I was terrified she was going to seduce you, that snowy night. Well, Rodney was the only man around here who didn't disappoint her – who lived up to her self-image. Apparently she is very sexy. Rodney said he was rather put off by his sensation that at that point in time – I sound like Nixon – she would fuck anybody. I wish he hadn't told me – even Frank doesn't know, and I hate having a secret from *him*.'

'Such beautiful scruples,' said I.

'Go ahead, mock. I deserve it, I guess.'

'My martyr. My Jeanne in the flames,' I said, hardly able to wait until I could take her to bed and discover how her new knowledge, her fresh corruption, had enriched her.

Yet we did divorce, in painful piecemeal, as did Maureen and Rodney. I moved to Nashua, but would return to Pierce Junction to visit the children, take Jeanne's temperature, and play my old games. One poker night, rather than let me drive back to Nashua full of beer, Rodney insisted that I sleep in his bachelor shack, up in the hills, at the end of a mile of dirt road. While waiting for my turn to use the bathroom, I saw a note carelessly left on his cluttered desk. The rounded upright handwriting, with its 'a's oddly like 'o's, struck me as momentously familiar; Audrey Lancaster had been the secretary of a conservation committee I had once served on. *Another fool's errand*, it read. *Did I misunderstand, or has Friar Lawrence goofed again? Now my van is dusty and my legs full of mosquito bites from an hour on your porch. Some damn bird in your woods was trying to deliver a message in clear English but couldn't quite make it out of birdsong. Yours, sort of. Yes?*

Unsigned. A blue-lined page torn, with an anger visible in the tearing, from a college notebook. A thumbtack hole where it had been pinned up outside. It brought me thrillingly close to Audrey, as close as we had been the night I had rested my palm on her haunch. She had come up that gloomy dirt road through the forest like a big smooth salmon upstream, and ignominiously driven back down again. Her literary allusion seemed more like Winifred, somehow.

When Rodney emerged innocently from the bathroom, wearing little-boy cotton pajamas and a fleck of toothpaste on his chin, I hated him as never in those years of entering his big house near the college, past the lawnmower and the oil cans in his garage, through the kitchen where he gobbled breakfast every day, past the shelf of his golf trophies, toward the mahogany guest bed. While some of us burned on the edges of life, insatiable and straining to see more deeply in, he sat complacently at the center and let life come to him – so much of it, evidently, that he could not keep track of his appointments.

Down in Nashua, as the Seventies dwindled into Jimmy Carter's inflation and malaise, I lost track of the ins and outs of life in Pierce Junction. The possibility that Maureen and I might get together on a respectable basis had been early dismissed by her. Too many children, too much financial erosion, too much water over the dam. 'Don't you see, Marty?' she told me. 'We've *done* it. We'd look at each other and all we'd see would be evidence of our *sin!*'

The quaint last word shocked me with the possibility that she – and Jeanne, and all the women – had been suffering in our sexual paradise, stressed and taxed by the divergence from monogamy. I felt insulted. So it was with, among other things, a pang of vengeful satisfaction that I heard of her sudden death, in a car driven late at night along Route 202 by, of all people, Spike Lancaster, a beefy, loud, hard-drinking restaurateur whose plain deficiencies had given Audrey, in our little set, a halo of forbearance. Spike and Audrey had nothing in common but bad eyesight. Maureen died, and he, the driver, came out of the crash with minor injuries and a rakish reputation that probably didn't hurt business in his roadside restaurant – called, actually, the Lucky Shamrock.

I could hardly believe that, after sublime us, Maureen could have taken up with this brute, this simpleton. Served her right, getting her neck broken, that slender neck springing with its pulse from a circle of summer sunburn. These ugly, unworthy thoughts lasted only a second, of course – a lightning flicker of amoral neurons before the gentle rain of decent sadness began. But her death, and this final scandal, with its black skidmarks and shattering of safety glass, did shut down Pierce Junction for me.

Jeanne and Frank married, and I edged into a second life, with a second wife and new children. My own children continued to grow, went to college, married, and moved away. I had fewer and fewer reasons to return; when I did, the town's geography, little changed, seemed to contain the same old currents, but the wires were different. The faces, and the old wormholes, if they still existed, were out of sight, running through younger lives. When I thought back to our hectic, somehow sacred heyday, it was, as I say, less in terms of the women closest to me than of those in the middle distance, relatively virginal, who had taken the siren call of the unknown with them as they disappeared over my horizon.

A mall had sprung up between Nashua and Pierce Junction, on the site of a dairy farm whose silver-tipped silos I still expected to see gleaming at that particular turn of the highway. Instead, there was this explosively fragmented glitter – chain stores in postmodern glass skins, and a vast asphalt meadow paved with cars. Intending to buy a grandchild a birthday present at one of those toy emporia with the queerly reversed 'R,' I was traversing the insistently musical reaches of an enclosed arcade lined, in its parody of an old-time Main Street, with windows of name-brand goods and dotted with underpatronized kiosks offering tinselly jewelry, exotic herbal teas, and candy and yogurt-coated pretzels in cloudy plastic bins. Suddenly I saw in the middle distance an unmistakable walk – splay-footed, wary, yet determinedly forward and, to my eyes, enticingly youthful. I ducked into a Gap outlet and, concealed amid shelves of softened denim and earthtone turtlenecks, gazed out as Audrey, plumper and gray but still supple, passed. The contact lenses that she was always losing had given way to cheerfully clunky thick glasses. She was squinting and smiling and talking with animation, moving that flexible mur-murous wide mouth of hers.

Her companion, wearing trousers and a feathery short white hairdo and a quilted down vest, for a moment seemed a complete stranger, a solemnly pout-ing small man. But then, with a stab of recognition that set off a senile stir of excitement behind my fly and jumped me a step farther back from the window, I saw; there was of course no mistaking the barrel-shaped owl body, the hooded dark eyes, the dainty extremities. Winifred. She and Audrey moved with the dreamy mutual submission of an old married couple. They were holding hands.

Transaction

In December of the year 197–, in the city of N—, a man of forty was walking toward his hotel close to the hour of midnight. The conference that had kept him in town had dispersed; he was more than a touch drunk; in his arms he carried Christmas presents for his loved ones – wife, children. At the edge of the pavement, beneath his eyes, bloomed painted young women, standing against the darkened shop fronts in attitudes that mingled expectancy and insouciance, vulnerability and guardedness, solitude and solidarity. A scattered army, was his impression, mustering half-heartedly in retreat. Neon syllables glowed behind them; an unlit sign, MASSAGE PARLOR, hung at second-story level, and his face, uptilted, received an impression of steam, though the night was as cold as the spaces between the stars.

A large Negress in a white fur coat drew abreast of him at a red light, humming. His eyes slid toward her; her humming increased in volume, was swelled from underneath, by a taunting suggestion of *la-di-da*, into almost a song. Fear fingered his heart. He shifted his paper Christmas bags to make a shield between him and this sudden, fur-coated, white-booted, melodious big body. The light broke; under the permission of green he crossed the avenue known as T— and walked up the hard, faintly tugging slant of sidewalk that would lead him to the voluminous anonymity of his hotel, the rank of silver elevator doors, the expectant emptiness of his room.

A glass office building floated above his shoulder, silent as an ice floe. Amid this deathly gray of winter and stone, a glistening confusion of contrary possibility was born in him, an incipient nest of color. In the unlit grated window of a corner drugstore, cardboard Magi were bringing their gifts. He turned left and circled the block, though his arms ached with his packages and his feet with the cold.

The routed but raffish army of females still occupied their corner and dim doorways beyond. Our passerby hesitated on the corner diagonally opposite, where in daytime a bank reigned amid a busy traffic of supplicants and emissaries, only to become at nightfall its own sealed mausoleum. He saw the prettiest of the girls, her white face a luminous child's beneath its clownish dabs of rouge and green, approached by an evidently self-esteeming young man, a rising insurance agent or racketeer, whose flared trouser-legs protruded beneath a camel-colored topcoat, correctly short. He talked to the girl earnestly; she listened; she looked diagonally upward as if to estimate something in the aspiring architecture above her; she shook her head. He repeated his proposition, bending forward engagingly; she backed away; he smartly turned and walked off.

Had it been a pack of schoolchildren, the others would have crowded around her, eager for details. But the other women ignored her, maintaining each her own vigil.

Seeing an approach having been made emboldened our onlooker to cross to their side of the avenue and to walk through the cloud of them again. His packages perhaps betrayed him; he was a comet returning. They recognized him. He felt caught up, for all the seasonal good will in his heart, in a warfare of caution and invisibility. His breath held taut against some fantastic hazard, he passed through the prime concentration, centered upon the luminous face of the child beauty. Only when the cloud thinned did he dare glance sideways, at an apparition in a doorway, who, the glance told him, was far from pretty – bony, her narrow face schoolteacherishly beaked – but who, even as he reproached himself, did accept his signal.

'Hi,' she said. A toothy white smile suddenly slashed the doorway shadows. With triggered quickness she came forward from her niche and at the same mechanical speed inserted her hand in the crevice between his body and his arm, among the rustling bags decorated with bells, conifers, snowmen.

He answered, 'Hi.' He felt his voice dip deep into a treasure of composure, warmth, even power. Her touch was an immense relief.

'Thirty O.K.?' she asked in a rapid whisper.

'Sure.' The back of his throat itched with silliness, which rose to counter the humorless, slithering urgency of her question.

She posed another: 'You got a place?'

He named the hotel, the R——, fearing it told too much about him – solid, square, past its prime.

Indeed, the name did seem to amuse her, for she repeated it, skipping with the same breath to put herself in step with him and tightening her grip on his arm. His clothes, layer upon layer, felt transparent. He plaintively accused, 'You don't like my hotel.'

'Why wouldn't I?' she asked, with that intimidating, soft-voiced rapidity. He saw that the stratagems, the coaxing ironies useful and instinctive in his usual life, would have small application in this encounter. I produce, you produce. Provocation had zero value.

He wanted to do the right thing. Would she expect to be taken to a bar? He had already drunk, he estimated, more than enough. And wouldn't it be to her profit to go to his room promptly and be done? She was a treasure so clumsily wrapped as to be of indeterminate size. Experimentally, he turned left, as on his prior circuit; she did not resist; together they crossed the avenue and climbed the hard little slant of pavement he had climbed before. Her grip tightened on his arm; he felt a smile break the mask of cold on his face. He was her prize; she, his. She asked, 'What's your name?'

Amid his sensations of cold and alcohol and pleasure at this body warm and strange and tugging against his, he imagined his real name would break the spell. He lied, 'Ed.'

She repeated it, as she had the name of the hotel, testing it in her mouth. Many names had passed through her mouth. Her voice, it seemed to him, had an East Coast edge without being indigenous to N—. She volunteered, 'Mine's Ann.'

He was touched to sense that she was not lying. He said, 'Hello, Ann.'

'Hello.' She squeezed his arm, so his mind's eye saw his bones. 'What do you do, travel for some company?' Her question and answer were one.

'Sure,' he said, and changed the subject. 'Am I walking too fast for you?' Something chalklike was coating his words. He mustn't, he told himself, be frightened of this woman; his fright would not serve either of them. Yet her presence nearly submerged his spirit in wonder. She loomed without perspective, like an abutment frozen in the headlights the moment after a car goes out of control. He glanced at her obliquely. City light had soaked into her face. Her long nose looked waxen. She was taller than the average woman, though still shorter than he. In his elementary school there had been a once-a-week penmanship teacher who had seemed ageless to him then but whose bony ranginess when she was young would have resembled Ann's.

She answered carefully. 'No. You're walking fine. Who are the presents for?'

His own question, he felt, had been subtly mocked. He answered hers mockingly: 'People.'

They did not talk again for some minutes.

The little paved rise crested. His hotel filled the block before them. In its grid of windows some burned; most were dark. Midnight had passed. The great building blazed erratically, like a ship going down. He said,

'There's a side entrance up this way.' She may have known this, but didn't indicate so. Had she been here before? Often? He could have asked, but did not; he did not ask, in retrospect, so many questions she might have willingly answered. For women, it turns out, always in retrospect, were waiting to be asked.

The side entrance was locked. The revolving door was chained.

Against them? Not only was Ed a stranger to the etiquette of prostitution, but hotels puzzled him. Was a hotel merely a store that sells rooms, or is it our watchdog and judge, with private detectives eyeing every corridor through dummy fire extinguishers, and lawyers ready to spring from the linen closets barking definitions of legal occupancy? They had to walk, Ann and Ed, another half-block in the interstellar cold and to brave the front entrance. The maroon-capped door-man, blowing on his hands, let them pass as if by a deliberate oversight. Mounting the stairs to the lobby, Ed was aware of the brass rods, slimmer than jet trails, more polished than presentation pens, that held the red carpet to the marble. He was aware of the warmth flowing down from the lobby and of, visible beneath her black maxicoat as she preceded him by a step, tall laced boots of purple suede. The lobby was calm. The cigar stand was shrouded for the night. Behind the main desk, men murmured into telephones and trans-posed coded numerals with the muffled authority of Houston manipulating a spacecraft. A few men in square gray suits, travelling men, rumpled but reluctant to be launched toward bed, stood about beneath the chandeliers. With his crackling packages and his bought woman packaged in black maxi and laced boots, Ed felt disadvantageously encumbered. His eyes rigidly ahead, he crossed to the elevator doors of quilted colorless metal. He pushed the Up button. The wait built tall in his throat before an arriving car flung back a door. It was theirs. No one at the control desk looked up. At the last second, as the doors sighed to close, two men in gray pushed in with them, and stared at Ann, and smiled. One man began to hum, like the Negress on the street.

Didn't Ann look like a wife? Didn't all young women dress like whores these days? She was plain, plainly dressed, severe, and pale. He could not quite look at her, or venture a remark, even as he inched closer to protect her from the strangers' gazing. The elevator grew suffocating with the exhalations of masculinity, masculinity inflated by booze. The humming grew louder, and plainly humorous. Perhaps an apparent age-difference had betrayed them, though Ed had always been told, by those who loved him, that he looked young for his years. One man shifted his weight. The other cleared his throat. Ed lifted his eyes to the indicator glow, as it progressed through the numbers 4, 5, and 6 and, after a yawning interval in which assault and murder might have been committed, halted at 7, his floor. As the two of them stepped out, she halted, not knowing whether to turn right or left. One of the men behind them called musically, 'Good night.'

Bastard. Buy your own whore.

*

'To the left,' he told her, when the elevator door had sucked shut. In a mirror set diagonally where the corridor turned, he imagined a spectator, a paid moral agent of some sort, watching them approach the turning. Then, after they turned, the agent – with his fat cigar and tinfoil badge – was transposed in a magical knight's move to where they had been, now watching them recede, Ed's back eclipsing his packages. Ann's maxi swung stiffly, a cloth bell tolling the corridor's guilty silence.

The key balked at fitting. He could not open the door to his room, which he had paid for. Struggling, blushing, he dropped a package, which his companion stooped to retrieve. That was good of her. This service free of charge. The key turned. The door opened into a dark still space as tidy and kind as a servant waiting up.

He held open the door for Ann to precede him, and in this gesture discovered his mood: mock courtesy. The hotel corridor, with its walls of no certain color and its carpet cut from an endless artificial tundra of maroon, somehow came with her, past his nose, into the room. The pallor of her face, momentarily huge, bounced his gaze to the window, its rectangle of diffuse city light flayed by Venetian blinds. As his eyes adjusted, the walls glowed. The package she had retrieved she set down on the gleam of a glass bureau top. He set the other packages down beside it; his arm ached in relief. He found the wall switch, but the overhead light was too bright. He could not look at her in such bright light. He brushed the switch off and groped at the base of the large ceramic lamp standing on the bureau top. This light, softer, showed her a distance away, standing by the bed, her hand on the second button of her long dark coat, undoing it; by this gesture of undoing she transposed his sense of her as packaged from the coat to the room itself, to the opaque plaster walls that contained her, to the fussy ceiling fixture like the bow at the top of a box. She was his, something he had bought. Yet she was alive, a person, unpredictable, scarcely approachable indeed. For his impulse to kiss her was balked by unstated barriers, a professional prohibition she radiated even as she smiled again that unexpected slash of a toothy smile and, after hesitating, as she had when stepping from the elevator door, handed him her coat – heavy, chill, black – to hang in the closet, which he did happily, his courtesy not altogether mock.

He turned. Who are you? he asked her, within himself. His apprehensions ricocheted confusedly, in the room's small space, off this other, who, standing in its center, simultaneously rendered it larger and many-sided and yet more shallow, as if she were a column faced with little mirrors. He stood motionless, perhaps also a column faced with mirrors – as in ballrooms, theatre lobbies, roller-skating rinks. Absurd, of course, to place two such glittering pillars so close together in so modest a room; but, then, perhaps in just such disproportion does sex loom amid the standardized furniture of our lives.

She moved a step. Something spilling from one of the packages attracted her: a book. She pulled it forth;

it was Blake's *Auguries of Innocence*, illustrated by Leonard Baskin woodcuts – a present for his wife, who in the early years of their marriage used to carve a woodcut as their annual Christmas card. Ann opened the pages, and the look of poetry on the page surprised her. 'What's it about?' she asked.

'Oh,' he said. 'It's about everything, in a way. About seeing a world in a grain of sand, and Heaven in a wild flower.' He heard a curious, invariable delay in the answers they made each other: tennis with sponge rackets. It might have been his thicknesses of alcohol. The brandy had been the worst mistake.

She let a page turn itself under her fingers, idle. 'I used to work in a library.'

'Where?' Under cover of her apparent interest in the book, he moved two steps to be behind her, and touched the zipper at the back of her sweater. It was magenta, wool, a turtleneck, somehow collegiate in quality, perhaps borrowing this quality from their bookish conversation. He thought of pulling the zipper and gingerly didn't dare; he thought of how, with any unbought woman, in such a sealed-off midnight room, hands and lips would have rushed into the vacuum of each other's flesh, sliding through clothes, ravenous for skin.

She answered his question reluctantly, not lifting her attention from the book. 'In Rhode Island.'

'What town?'

Her attention lifted. 'You know Rhode Island?'

'A little. We used to have some friends we'd visit in Warwick.'

'The library was in Pawtucket.'

'What's Pawtucket like?'

She said, 'Not bad. It's not all as ugly as what you see from Route One.'

He pulled down her zipper, a little pink zipper, enough to let her head slip through. Her cervical vertebrae and some down at her neck's nape were bared. 'Did you like it,' he asked, 'working in the library?' Under his fingertips her nape down tingled; he felt her expecting him to ask how she had got from the library into this profession. He refused to ask, discovering a second mood, after mock courtesy, of refusal. For hadn't she, silently, by some barrier in her manner, refused him a kiss?

She moved away from his touch. 'Yeah, I did.' She was young and lean, he saw, a brunette, her hair crimpy and careless and long. Not only her nose but her teeth were too big, so that her lips, in fitting over them, took on an earnest, purposeful expression; she appeared to him, again, as a schoolteacher, with a teacher's power of rebuke. He laughed, rebelling – laughed at her moving away from him so pensively. As the outdoor cold melted out of his body, the alcohol blossomed into silliness, foaming out of him like popcorn from a popper. Acting the bad boy, he pulled off his overcoat, suit coat, and tie; ashamed of his silliness and the fear it confessed, he went toward her as if for an embrace but instead tugged the hem of her sweater out of her skirt and pulled it upward. Understanding, surrendering, she shook her head to loosen her hair and raised her arms; the sweater came free. Lifting it from her hands, he saw she had long oval nails, painted with clear polish. Her bra was severely white, hospital-plain. This surprised him, in an era when even the primmest of suburban women wore coquettish, lace-trimmed underwear. And he was additionally surprised that, though his whore's shoulders were bony and bore the same glazed pallor as her face, her breasts were a good size, and firm. Amid the interlock of these small revelations an element clicked apart and permitted him to place his arms around her hard shoulders and tighten them so that the winter chill and stony scent of her hair flowed from the top of her head into his nostrils. His voice leaped from the cliff of her ting-ling hair; he asked, 'You want your thirty now or after?'

'Whichever,' she said, then – a concession, her first, possibly squeezed from her by alarm, for his extreme reasonableness did, he perceived, resemble insanity – 'after.'

'So you're a librarian,' he sighed.

His relief must have been too huge, too warm; she pushed his chest away with iron fingertips. 'Why don't you go into the bathroom,' she suggested, using a disciplinarian's deceptive softness of tone, 'and' – she lightly tapped his fly with the back of her hand – 'wash them up.'

Them! The idea of designating his genitals a population, a little gabbling conclave of three, made his silliness soar and his complementary mood of refusal deepen, darken toward cruelty. With the deliberateness of an insult or of a routine of marriage he sat in the hotel armchair and took off his shoes and socks, tucking the socks in the shoes. Then he stood and, insolent but for the trembling of his fingers and the wave of alcohol tipping him forward, unbuttoned his shirt, pulled off his undershirt, managed the high-wire two-step of trouser removal. He was aware of her motionless by the bed, but could not look directly at her, to gauge the image she was reflecting, or to catch a glimmer of himself. She was a pillar of black facets. A wave of alcohol must then have broken over him, for he lost her entirely, and found himself standing naked before the bathroom basin, on tiptoe, soaping his genitals above the lunar radiance of its porcelain and still smiling at the idea of calling them *them*.

As he washed, the concepts her directive had planted – dirt, germs, disease, spoilage – infiltrated the lathery pleasure, underminingly. His tumescence, he observed, was slight. He rinsed, splashing cold water with a cupped hand, dried himself with a towel, tucked the towel modestly about his waist, and walked out into the other room.

Ann was naked but for her boots. Purple suede, they were laced up to her knees. Were they too tedious to unlace? Was this a conventional turn-on? A put-down? An immense obscure etiquette whose principles hulked out of the city night to crowd them into this narrow space of possible behavior blocked him from asking why she had kept them on or whether she might take them off. As if another woman in undressing had revealed a constellation of moles or a long belly scar, he was silent, and accepted the boots along with the slim waxen whiteness of the rest of her, a milk snake with one black triangular marking.

He had worn the towel as provocation, hoping she might untuck it for him. His current mistress, most graciously, unlaced his shoes, and stayed on her knees. But Ann's sole move was to tuck back her hair as if to keep it clear of the impending spatter of dirty business. He let his towel drop and held her, with no more pressure than causes a stamp to adhere to an envelope. He in bare feet, she still in boots, they came closer in height than on the street, and his prick touched her belly just above the black triangle. She backed off sharply: 'You're icy!'

'I washed like you told me to.'

'You could have used warm water.'

'I did, I thought.'

She bent down, but to pick up the towel. She handed it to him. 'Dry yourself, can't you?'

'Jesus, you're fussy.' He must counterattack. 'How about you?' he asked. 'Don't you want to use the bathroom?'

'No.'

'Don't you need to go wee-wee or anything, standing around on the street for hours?'

'No, thank you.'

'It's a perfectly good bathroom.'

Just when he had figured her as mechanically one-track, she changed her mind. 'O.K. I will.' She went into the bathroom. She closed the door! So he couldn't watch. No free pleasures, he saw, was one of the rules.

Naked, he sat on the bed, picked the Blake from the
bureau top, and read,

> The Lamb misus'd breeds Public strife
> And yet forgives the Butcher's Knife.
> The Bat that flits at close of Eve
> Has left the Brain that won't Believe.

The toilet flushed; the faucets purred. She emerged
still wearing those bothersome, unlovely boots, and
gave his limp penis a glance he thought scornful. Only
the alcohol helped him ask, 'Want to lie down?'

Without voicing assent, she sat on the bed stiffly
and let herself be pulled horizontal. Her skin felt too
young, too firm and smooth. Passing his hands down
the mathematically perfect curves of her sides and buttocks, he calculated that the journey of happiness from
these hands into his head and from there down his
spine to his prick was, rendered tenuous and errant by
his drunkenness, too long. He stroked her breasts, so
firmly and finely tipped as to feel conical. His sense of
breasts had been shaped by his overflowing wife. Once
when she was nursing one of their babies he had sucked
a mouthful of milk from her and, not swallowing, filled
her own mouth with it, so she, too, could know the
taste. By comparison this kid's tits were so firm as to
feel unkind. Her belly was flat, with the sheen of a
tabletop beneath his fingers, and the hair of her pussy
was thick, stiff, brushlike. The first time he had slept
with a woman not his wife, she had been a mutual
friend, a shy and guilty woman who had undressed out

of sight and come back to him wearing her slip over nothing; touched, her pussy beneath the nylon had been so startlingly soft he had exclaimed, 'Oh,' and she with him – '*Oh!*' – as if together on a walk they had simultaneously sighted a rare flower, or a sun-splashed bed of moss.

Ann, stroked, took this as the signal to set her own hand, cool and unfeeling, on his prick. Too rapidly she twitched the loose skin back and forth; he huddled inside his drunkenness and giggled.

'What's so funny?' she asked.

'You're so nice,' he lied. It came to him that the part-time penmanship teacher would sometimes touch him, reaching over his shoulder to roughly grab his wrist and push and pull his hand back and forth to give him the idea of not writing with his wrist and fingers but with his forearm.

Ann sat up to continue with better leverage her attack on his prick. It tickled, twittered, and stung; his consciousness drew back, higher, as a man climbs higher into the bleachers for a more analytical view of the game. Either this girl had no aptitude for her profession, or love cannot be aped. She flicked her head haughtily, stopped her futile agitation of his penis, put her mouth to his ear, and whispered with that slithering urgency she affected, 'Do you like me?'

'Sure.'

'Well, *look* at it.' She flipped it. He looked. It lay sideways, enviably asleep. She asked, 'How long do you expect me to keep at it?'

'Not long,' he said pleasantly; her fingers, inert, felt

pleasant. 'You can go now. I'll get you your thirty dollars. Sorry I'm such a flop.'

Her face, softer in shadow, pondered. 'Ed, look. I'll stay, but it'll take a little more.'

'How much more, for how long?' The prompt specificity of his question took her aback. He helped her, though he was new at this and she wasn't. 'How about one hour,' he proposed, 'for thirty more? In an hour the drinks should wear off enough so I can get it up. I'm sorry, I'd like to fuck you, I really would.'

Displeasingly, her whisper hoarsened, becoming theatrical, seductive. 'How about being Frenched? Like that? For twenty more I'll French you. Would you like that, Ed?'

Naked and lazy, he shifted position on the bed. Impotent or not, he was the boss. In daylight transactions he hated haggling; but this was different. She was so young she could be teased. Her youth furthermore made her an enemy. For this was the era of student revolts, of contempt for the old virtues, of energy-worship. 'Twenty more!' he protested. 'That makes eighty all told. You'll bankrupt me. Why would a nice girl like you want to come in off the street and bankrupt some poor john?'

She ignored his irony, asking with her closest approximation to true excitement, 'How much cash you got?'

'Want me to count it?'

'Don't you *know?*'

'Like I said, I was Christmas shopping. Jesus. Hold on. Don't go away mad.'

He hoisted himself from the bed, located his pants draped on the back of the plush-covered armchair, found the wallet within them, and counted the bills. One hundred ten, one twenty, twenty-two, three. 'O.K.,' he told her. 'Eighty-four dollars total. I can just spare eighty. That's for one hour, starting now, not when you came in, and including you Frenching me. Agreed?'

'O.K.'

He considered asking that she remove her boots in the bargain; but he feared she would put a price on that, and, though he could inflict upon her the suspense of haggling, he would always end, he knew, by meeting her price. Also, there was a mystery about the boots that made him squeamish. To watch him count his money, Ann had lifted herself on the bed, up on her knees like a little girl playing jacks. Ed touched her cold shoulder, silently bidding her to hold the position, and then fit himself into her pose so a nipple met his mouth. He lapped, sucked, rubbed. She said, 'Ow.'

He removed his mouth an inch. 'What do you mean, "Ow"?'

'Didn't you shave today?'

'Not since this morning. Can you notice?'

'*Feel* it,' she said.

He rubbed his own chin and upper lip. 'That can't hurt,' he told her.

'It does.'

He looked up, and her face and torso held a stillness that for the first time, it seemed to his sheepish sense, admitted a glimmer of erotic heat into the frozen space between them. Since he could not impress her by anger, not being angry, nor by being himself, since he had sold himself short by applying to her at all, he would act out compliance. He would overwhelm her with docility. 'I'll go shave, then.'

She did not object.

He asked, before moving, 'Will the shaving time come out of my hour?'

She said, not even audibly bored, her voice was so flat, 'If you're going to do it, Ed, do it.'

Standing again above the basin's bright moon, he felt his genitals stir, sweeten, with the idea of it: the idea of shaving, so domestically, to oblige this ungrateful stringy whore in the next room, street-cold still clinging to her skin. When he returned, his cheeks gleaming, his loins bobbling, she observed his excitement and in an act of swift capture produced from somewhere (her boot?) a prophylactic and snapped it into place around his semi-erect prick and lay on her back with legs spread. Though he held stiff enough to enter her and momentarily think, *I'm fucking this woman*, the scent and pinch of rubber, and an inelasticity within her, and something unready and resentful in himself – *and she couldn't care less*, was the successor thought – combined to dwindle him. His few dud thrusts were like blank explosions by whose flash he exposed the full extent of their interlocked abasement. Apologetically, he withdrew, and tugged off the condom and, not knowing upon what hotel surface he could place it without offending her stern standards of hygiene, held the limp little second skin dangling in his hand as he stretched out sorrowfully beside her defeated female form. 'Those things cost, you know,' she said.

What shall we do? Ann lay in a sulk, but he imagined a rift in the surface of her impatience, a ledge to which he might cling. With his free hand (the other arm tucked back under his head so the condom hung cleanly over the edge of the bed) he stroked the long cold curve of her side, illumined by the window with Venetian blinds. He told her, 'You're gorgeous.'

As if equivalently, she asked him, 'You married?'

'Sure.' She might have thought this was the door, at last, to the confident intimacy between them that he, she must now realize, needed. But it opened instead on a cul-de-sac, the marriage that had put them here; they lay inside his wife's sexual nature as in a padded, bolted dungeon. Ed could have attempted to share this vision with Ann, but attempted more simply to return the friendliness she seemed now willing, if only out of fear of being trapped with him forever, to concede. He asked her, 'How old are you?'

'Twenty-two.' A new tone, bitter. Did she feel so soon blighted, hopelessly fallen? Her beakish, colorless profile lifted above him, into the square cloud of light leaking from the circumambient city. 'You?'

'Fortyish.'

'The prime of life.'

'Depends.' He rubbed his mouth across her nipples, then his cheek, asking, 'That smooth enough?'

'It's better.'

'You like it? I mean, normally, does it leave you cold, turn you off, or what?'

She didn't answer; he had trespassed, he realized, into another dark clause of their contract: her pleasure was not at issue. Able to do no right, and therefore no wrong, he slid his face from her breast to her belly and, as she lay back, past her wiry pubic bush to her thigh. He rested his head there. He laid the condom on the sheet beside her waist and with his hands parted her thighs; she complied guardedly. An edge of one boot scraped his ear as he moved his head back, as when reading a telephone book, to see better. Between her legs lay darkness. He stroked her mons veneris, and the tendoned furred hollows on either side; he ran his thumb the length of her labia, parted them, softly sank his thumb in the cleft in which, against all tides of propriety and reasonableness, a little moisture was welling. He withdrew his thumb and inserted his middle finger, his thumb finding socket on her anus.

The diffuse light was gathering to his eyes now, and he saw the silver plane of the inner thigh turned to the window, and the same light sliding on his tapering forearm and moving wrist, and the two bright round corners of her buttocks beneath, and the pale meadow of her foreshortened belly, the taut hills of her breasts, the far underside of her chin. From the angle of her chin she was gazing out the window, at the strange night sky of N—, like the sky of no other city, brown and golden, starless, permeated with the aureole of its own swamp-fire static. Through the warp and blur of alcohol the inner configurations of her cunt, the granular walls, the elusive slippery hooded central hardness, began to cut an image in his mind, and to give him a jeweller's intent, steady joy.

She spoke. Her voice floated hoarse across the silver terrain of her body. Her words were most surprising. 'Do you ever,' she asked, hesitating before finishing, 'use your tongue?'

'Sure,' he said.

Bending his face to her aperture, he felt blow through his skull the wind of all those who had passed this way before him. Yet, though no doubt men had flooded this space with their spunk and Heaven knew what perversities had been visited upon her by strangers struggling to feel alive, her cunt did not taste of anything; it was clean of any scent, even that of deodorant, and its surround of brushlike hair had the prickly innocence of a child's haircut or of the pelt of a young nocturnal omnivore such as a raccoon. He regretted that in the politics of their positioning his mouth did not come at it upside down but more awkwardly, frontally, with his body trailing between and beyond her legs like an unusably heavy kite tail, and with his neck bent back to the point of aching. Seeking to penetrate, his tongue tensed behind it the entire length of his spine. Opening his eyes, he saw a confused wealth of light-struck filaments that might be vegetation on Mars, or mildew under the microscope.

A miracle, she seemed to be moving. In response. She was. She was heaving her hips to help his tongue go deeper. He suspected a put-on. He was willing to believe that he could arouse his shy, plump mistress:

he was a popularizer of astronomy and she his research assistant, and when she would swing her crotch around to his face its spread wet halves would swamp his consciousness like a star map of both hemispheres, not only the stars one saw but the Southern constellations – Lupus, Phoenix, Fornax. But this waxen street-lily surely was beyond him, another galaxy, far out. Yet the girl lifted her pelvis and rotated it and forcefully sighed. She had been so unemphatic and forbidding in all else, he doubted she would fake this. The thought that he was giving her pleasure invited cruelty, as a clean sheet invites mussing. His prick was becoming a weapon; in the air beyond the foot of the bed he felt it enlarging, presenting more surface to the air. He pulled himself up, still drunker than he should be, his shaved chin wet with her, and asked, 'Didn't you say you'd French me?'

As if abruptly awakened, Ann seemed to find her body heavy. She pushed her weight up onto her arms as he relaxed his length into the trough of warmth she had left on the narrow, single bed. She tucked back her hair from her temples. She straightened his stiffened prick with her fingers and bent her lips to the glans. Her lips made a silent *O* as he pushed up. Her head bobbed in and out of the cloud of light. She moved her mouth up and down as rapidly and ruthlessly as she had her hand; he watched with drowsy amazement, wondering what book of instructions she had read. This fanciful impression, that she had learned to perform this service from a manual and was performing it mechanically, an application of purely exterior knowledge, with none of the empathy for the other sex that Eros in blindness bestows, excited him, so he did not lose his erection to his schoolmarm's rote blowing. How many times a night did she do this? He saw, dismally but indulgently, his prick as a product, mass-produced and mass-consumed in a few monotonous ways. Poor dear child. With a distant affection he let his fingertips drift to one nipple and followed its sympathetic rise and fall; so Galileo followed the rhythmic radiance of Jupiter's revolving satellites. Hard and small and perfect and glossy and cool, her nipple. Hers, an outpost of her nervous system. He was growing accustomed to her, her temperature, texture, manner, pulse, and saliva. His hard prick glittered when her profile did not eclipse it.

Time slipped by for him, but a meter in her head told her she had Frenched twenty dollars' worth. Swiftly, as a fisherman transfers the kicking fish to the net, she lifted the circle of her lips from his phallus, retrieved the condom from the bedsheet, deftly rerolled it, slipped it down upon his cock, and set herself astride, handsome and voracious in silhouette. She told him, with a trace of her old slithering, too-practiced urgency – modified in tone, however, by something unpracticed, young, experimental, and actually interested – 'We'll try it with me on top.' She lowered herself carefully, and he was inside her. Magnetically his finger-tips had never left her nipple.

'That's a good way,' he told her, just to say something, so she wouldn't feel utterly alone.

She moved her cunt and her body with it up and

down with the same unfeeling presto that must be, he deduced, the tempo most men like; how had he been misled into languorous full pulls and voyeuristic lingering? Too many prefatory years, he supposed, of fantasy and masturbation. *Mr Push-pull lives in here*, he remembered his penmanship teacher shouting to the class, 'in here' being the circle she had had them pen, in wet ink on blue-lined paper, with rigid wrists and forearms.

Though Ann's fucking felt like an attack, his prick held its own, and his hypnotic touch on her nipple also held. They were a strange serene boat, its engine pumping, gliding it could be forever through the glowing tan fog of the city night. With his other hand, again to let her know she was not wholly alone with the mechanical problem she was being paid to solve, he patted, then pushed her bottom. He thought, *I haven't fucked a woman this young for years*, and knew he was home. The canal lock had lifted, scenic point in the mountain pass had been attained, it was all downhill, he would have to come. The girl was virtually jumping now, out of a squat and back into it. Her boots were rough on his sides, her hair swung like a mop, her skin felt cool as a snake's: never mind, he would come, he would give it to her, the gift we are made to give, the seething scum the universe exists to float.

She squatted deep. His sleepy prick released a little shivery dream. Not a thumping come, but distinct and, for such a drunk, triumphant. Her shoulders and face were above him, dark, as the madonna in the icon is dark in that Russian movie where the damned hero attempts to pray.

But her darkness held a smile. She was above him like a mother nursing, darkness satisfied and proud, having been challenged and found not wanting.

'Oh, thank you,' he said. '*Thank* you. Sorry to have made you work so hard. *Sorry* to be so much trouble. Usually I come like a flash. My wife bitches about it.'

She did not bother to doubt this. There was no way he could win promotion from her classroom of the sexually defective. Indeed, had he not shown that only the most patient manipulation could enroll him among fornicators? Ann lifted her loins from his, with a delicate shrug of disentanglement – a giantess wading through muck on her knees. A novel sensation told him that she was not carrying his seed away with her, as his wife or mistress would. Rather, she had sealed it in at its source: sticky consequences. He disdained to remove the condom. She had enlisted him in a certain hostility toward the third member of their party, the pivotal presence in the room, though silent – his willful, erratic prick. Stew in your own juice.

Ann, too, acted lazy. Instead of wading on, out of his narrow bed, she lay down beside him in her boots. He felt why: it was warm here, and enclosed, and now she knew him, and was not frightened of him. He asked her, 'Aren't you anxious to get back out on the street?' He giggled, as if the joke were still on himself. 'And get away,' he continued, 'from these awful out-of-town husbands who are too drunk to fuck decently?'

She mistook him, still viewing him as a conquest. Absurd in her booted nakedness, she cuddled against him and said in the slithering breathy voice of her propositions, 'If you paid me enough I could stay all night. I bet you don't have enough money for me to stay all night.'

'I bet too I don't,' he told her soberly.

'For another thirty you might talk me into it.' Had she seen into his wallet? Or did she just know that all men are cheats?

He calculated: if the alcohol wore off, and he got a few hours' sleep, he could manage one more piece of ass; but then getting her out of here in the morning light, through the bustle of breakfast trays and suitcases, loomed as a perilous campaign. The men in the elevator had told him that she somehow looked like a whore. With her in this narrow bed with him he'd sleep badly and drag through the rest of the day. Not worth it. He told her, 'Honest, Ann, I don't have thirty more. I don't have *any* more.'

He stared down into her face for the seconds it took her to realize she was being spurned. His fear now was that she would offer to stay free. She sat up. He sat up on the edge of the bed with her. She waved her hand, as if to touch (but she did not touch) his penis, shrunken, wearing the trailing white prophylactic like an old-fashioned nightcap. *And Ma in her kerchief, and I in my cap . . .*

She asked, 'You gonna keep that as a souvenir?'

He asked, 'You want it back?'

'No, Ed. You can keep it.'

'Thanks. I keep saying "Thanks" to you, you notice?'

'I hadn't noticed.' She stood, her buttocks fair as Parian marble. 'Mind if I use your john before I go?'

'No, please do. Please.'

'Don't want to keep you from your beauty sleep.' But even this mild revelation of injury must have tasted unprofessional, passing her lips, for she relented and, gesturing again at the sheath on his prick, offered, 'Want me to flush that for you?'

'No. It's mine. I want it.'

She gathered some clothes, and he regretted afterwards that he had not pressed into his memory these last poses of her naked body. But a wave of blankness was emitted by the still-operant alcohol and ended by the soft slam of the bathroom door. Delicately he pulled off the condom and held it, pendulous, laden, while debating where to set it. At home he was hyperconscious of wineglass and water stains on furniture; but here, looking for a coaster, he saw only an ashtray. Removing the matches, he laid the sheath in it. She was taking her time in the bathroom. He picked up the Blake and tried to resume where he had left off. He couldn't find the place; instead his eye was taken by the typographical clasps of

> Every Morn & every Night
> Some are Born to sweet delight.
> Some are Born to sweet delight,
> Some are Born to Endless Night.

What was she doing in the bathroom? Did he hear her gargle and spit? He read on, more lines that also seemed too simple:

> We are led to Believe a Lie
> When we see not Thro' the Eye
> Which was Born in a Night to perish in a Night
> When the Soul Slept in Beams of Light.

He didn't understand this, nor why Blake hadn't bothered to make the lines scan.

Ann emerged from the bathroom wearing the purple boots, her antiseptically white bra, and the maxiskirt whose shade he had not observed before (charcoal). She glanced around for her sweater; he spotted its magenta spilled at the foot of the bed and held it out to her with a courtesy mocked by his total nakedness. She took it without a smile and pulled it over her head. She needed more fun in her life; in a better world his function might have been to brighten her gray classroom with a joke or two. She awkwardly reached behind her; he darted to her back and pulled up the zipper, covering her three cervical vertebrae and the faint dark down. In a serious voice he asked, 'Want me to get dressed and escort you out of the hotel?'

'No, Ed. I can find my way. I'll be all right.'

'All alone?'

She did not accept his invitation to say that she was always alone.

'I hate to think of you going back to stand around on that cold corner where it says Massage Parlor.'

To this, too, any reply would have been playing his game.

He chose to understand that she was eager to return, to the street of others grosser and more potent than he. You whore. You poor homely whore. You don't love me, I don't love you. 'What do you do in the day?' he asked.

That she answered surprised him, as did her answer. 'Take care of my kid.'

'You have a kid?' His sense of her underwent a revolution. Those small hard nipples had given milk; that brisk cunt had lent passage to a baby's head.

She nodded. The climate around her was exactly that as when she had answered, 'Twenty-two.' A central fact had been taken from her. Of the many possible questions, the one he asked, with stupid solicitude, was, 'Who's taking care of it now?'

'A baby-sitter,' Ann said.

What color was the baby-sitter? What color was the child? What about its future schooling? When are you going back to the library? How do you get out of this? How do I? He said, 'Your money. We got to get you your money.'

He went to his pants and picked the wallet from them too swiftly; the thin wedge of a hangover headache was inserted with the motion. 'Thirty,' he said, counting off tens to steady himself, 'and then thirty more for staying the hour, and twenty for the Frenching. Right? And then let's add ten for the baby-sitter. Ninety. O.K.?' Handing her the bills, he inspected her smile; it was not as wide as the smile she had brought forward from the doorway. An extra ten might have widened it, but he held it back, and instead said, to win her denial, 'Sorry I was such a difficult customer.'

She considered her answer deliberately; she was not an easy grader. 'You weren't a difficult customer, Ed. I've had lots worse, believe me. Lots worse.' Her lingering on this thought felt irritatingly like a request for sympathy.

'Pass with push, huh?' he said.

The joke didn't seem to register; perhaps by the time she had gone to high school the phrase had disappeared. She lifted her skirt and tucked the folded bills into one of her boots. Her boots were her bank, no wonder she wouldn't remove them. Still, by keeping them on, she had held off a potential beauty in him – in him and her together, naked, with the bare feet of animals made in the image of Blake's angels. 'I hate thinking,' he said, 'of you walking down that long corridor all by yourself.'

'I'll be all right, Ed.' Her saying his false name had become a nagging. As she put on her heavy all-concealing coat, he felt her movements were slowed by the clinging belief that he would relent and ask her to spend the night.

Naked, he dodged past her to the door. Her coat as he passed breathed the chill of outdoors onto his skin. 'O.K., Ann. Here we go. Thank you very much. You're great.'

She said nothing, merely tensed – her long nose wax-white, her eyelids the color of crème de menthe –

in expectation of his opening the door. As he reached for the knob, his hand appeared to him a miracle, an intricate marvel of bone and muscle and animating spirit. An abyss of loss seemed disclosed in the wonder of such anatomy. Her body, breathless and proximate, participated in the wonder; yet, anxious to sleep and seal himself in, he could not think of anything to do but dismiss this body, this wild flower.

The turn and click of the knob came like the snap of a bone breaking. He opened the door enough to test the emptiness of the corridor, but while he was still testing she pushed around him and into the hall. 'Hey,' he said. 'Goodbye.' Forgive me, help me, adore me, screw me, forget me, carry me with you into the street.

Ann turned in surprise, recalled to duty. She whispered, from afar, ''Bye,' and gave him half of her slash of a smile, the half not turned to the future. With that triggered quickness of hers she turned the corner and was gone. Her steps made no retreating sound on the hotel carpet.

Ed closed the door. He put across the safety chain. He took the prophylactic from the ashtray into the bathroom, where he filled it full of water, to see if it leaked. The rubber held, though it swelled to a transparent balloon in which water wobbled like life eager within a placenta. Good girl. A fair dealer. He had not given her a baby, she had not given him venereal disease.

What she had given him, delicately, was death. She had made sex finite. Always, until now, it had been too much, bigger than all systems, an empyrean as absolute as those first boyish orgasms, when his hand would make his soul pass through a bliss as dense as an ingot of gold. Now, at last, in the prime of life, he saw through it, into the spaces between the stars. He emptied the condom of water and brought it with him out of the bathroom and in the morning found it, dry as a husk, where he had set it, on the glass bureau top among the other Christmas presents.